THE COWGIRL WHO LOVED HORSES

QUEENS OF MONTANA, BONUS BOOK 5

VANESSA GRAY BARTAL

DRY CREEK PRESS

Cecily Blake sat on the fencepost and willed herself not to cry. In the past few months her life had been turned upside down, and now it was falling apart. If she didn't figure something out fast, she stood to lose everything her family had built for generations. The problem was that she had no solutions. She had spent her life doing as she pleased with no thought to how their business was run. Now she deeply regretted all the wasted years of selfishness.

A truck pulled up behind her and came to a stop, but she didn't turn to look. She knew it was one of the Henshaw's workers and she had no desire to talk, even if she did appear rude.

An undeniably male presence appeared beside her and rested his elbows on the fence. "Watcha staring at?" the man asked.

Cecily nearly fell off the fence in shock, but she covered her surprise and spoke calmly. "Hello, Marcus." She hadn't expected Marcus Henshaw himself to come.

He tipped his hat to her. "Cecily."

"Did all of your ranch hands run off or die?" she asked.

He gave her a wry smile. "Believe it or not I occasionally do some work myself."

She nodded. Everyone knew Marcus was a hard worker. Ever

since he graduated from college, he had a passion to make his ranch even more of a success than it already was. "Sort of like the guy who owns Boardwalk buying up all the rest of the board," she said.

"My favorite piece is the car," he said.

She was surprised he had picked up on her Monopoly reference. Lately she had been blurting whatever crossed her mind without running it through a filter first, and when it happened, most people stared at her in silent confusion.

"I like the dog," she said. Her mind conjured the image of the little metal dog, and she looked off toward the distance as she remembered afternoons spent playing Monopoly with Kitty and Dante. She never won. *It's like a metaphor for my life now. The stakes are higher, and I'm still losing.*

"Are you ready?" Marcus asked. His gentle tone grated on her nerves. She didn't want pity, especially not from one of the high and mighty Henshaws--the highest and mightiest Henshaw, no less.

She nodded curtly.

He offered his hand to help her down, but she ignored it and jumped off on her own. She brushed at the seat of her pants and led him to the entry of the corral.

He cleared his throat, clearly uncomfortable. "I sure am sorry about the trouble your family has been having lately."

She nodded curtly again in acknowledgement of his sentiment. "We'll manage. Congratulations on your engagement."

"Where did you hear that rumor? I'm not engaged."

She paused and looked at him with some of her old self returning to her. Once upon a time she had loved nothing better than neighborhood gossip. Now since they had become the main source of gossip she had lost her taste for it. "You're not?"

He shook his head. "We're still dating, same as we have been off and on for the last few years now."

She shook her head. "Sorry. Don't know how I got it so mixed up." But she did. She only half listened to people when they talked now; her mind was too much on her own problems to be involved with anyone else. She probably wouldn't have paid any attention to the chatter about Marcus and his girlfriend except for the fact that she found them fascinating. Marcus was their local celebrity. His family had more money than anyone she knew. He was handsome, charming, and well educated. The fact that he was dating a beauty queen only added to his mystique. She had always watched from a disinterested distance. He was six years older than her, and the conversation they were having right now was the first one they'd ever shared.

They reached the opening of the pen. "Here we are," she said. "It's probably best if you back your truck in. This guy has a temper."

Marcus nodded. He had been studying her suspiciously since he arrived and what he saw disturbed him. She was nothing like the Cecily he had watched grow up for so many years. She had always been a spirited and flighty little thing. He used to think there was nothing between her ears but cotton. True, he had never *really* known her, but he knew her in the way people know all their neighbors. She was his kid brother Mathew's age. There weren't a lot of people in these parts. They were a tight knit group, and it would have been impossible for Cecily to escape his notice. Plus he had to admit she was a pretty kid, and she always had been. Her mother was of Spanish descent. Cecily and her brother, Dante, received her dark complexion and hair. Cecily's hair flowed thickly down to the middle of her back, and she had a pleasant, shapely figure.

Today she wasn't the spirited girl from his memory, though. She was sad, broken, and afraid. He felt sorry for her, and he wished there was something he could do, but she was obviously proud. He smiled. He liked a girl with pride and spirit. His smile fled and he shook his head. No wonder he and Lacey weren't engaged. He couldn't seem to stop his eye from roaming, even to a child. He remembered Cecily's birth, for crying out loud, only a couple of months after Mathew's. He grimaced. What was wrong with him?

He backed the truck up to the pen and exited the truck to open the trailer. He knew Cecily had no idea he was paying above market price for the bull, and he would never tell her. It was one small way to help a neighbor, and it was a small price to pay because it was a good bull. His thoughts distracted him, so it took a split second for the small scream to register. When it did, he whirled to face the pen and his blood ran cold. Somehow in her attempt to open the gate Cecily had dropped onto the wrong side of the fence. The very large, very angry bull was now bearing down on her, and she was frozen in fear.

Action before thought had become his creed after so many years of ranch life. He swooped her up with one arm and jerked her out with such force they both toppled backwards. She landed on top of him and they froze, stunned from the possible danger she had faced. Then her face crumpled and she started to cry.

Marcus stared at the top of her head in consternation. What was he to do with her now? Gingerly he reached out his hand and smoothed it over her head. She rested her forehead on his chest and balled up his shirt in her fists.

"There now, it will be all right." He said it awkwardly because of course it wouldn't be all right. Her future was grim, and everyone knew it.

She sat up and looked at him. The sight of her sad little tear-streaked face did something to his heart, and now action before thought was his undoing as he moved his hands to cup her face and drew her forward for a kiss.

When their lips met, it was as if something was unleashed in both of them. For her part she was most likely seeking the comfort and security his embrace offered. That was easily explained and understood. What bothered him most was his headlong response to her. His last rational thought before he gave over to the kiss entirely was that he had never lost himself so completely in a kiss with anyone. Then she twined her fingers in his hair to tug him closer, and he turned off his mind completely.

CHAPTER 1

Cecily stood at the grave, dry-eyed and full of grief. She hadn't known him well, but it was always a shock when someone her age died. Or she supposed it would be; this was the first time it had ever happened.

Beside her Maggie Chapman was weeping hysterically while her sisters tried in vain to comfort her. On her other side, Mrs. Henshaw was crying with equal passion and volume. It was almost like a strange competition between the two women who had loved him most. Cecily gave herself a mental shake. What a terrible thought for her to have about two people who were experiencing such profound grief.

She felt eyes on her, and she knew without looking to whom they belonged. When she lifted her head, she stared into the hollow, empty eyes of Marcus Henshaw. No matter how hard she tried she couldn't look away. She felt his grief like a physical thing. Beside him stood his girlfriend looking beautiful and perfect, even in her grief. She clutched his arm, but he made no move to touch her in return. Instead he stared unblinkingly at Cecily, as if trying to convey a message, and she knew what it was.

He needed her. She had no idea how she knew, but she knew. They hadn't spoken one word since the strange and passionate kiss they had shared almost two years ago, but he watched her whenever they happened to meet, which wasn't often. As for her, she had tried to push him from her mind, but nothing worked. She dated occasionally, but none of the kisses she shared with other men equaled that one kiss she had shared with Marcus. She told herself she was too busy to care. The ranch required more and more of her time and energy these days, and she threw herself into it with relish. Anything to get away from her horrible loneliness.

Now she did silent battle with herself as people started to filter away. She had intended to go to the graveside service and go home. But now, with Marcus still staring beseechingly across the grave at her, she felt compelled to go to the Henshaw's house. She didn't want to, but she had to make sure he was all right.

Finally they were the last people at the graveside, and still he didn't look away. His girlfriend, who had followed his parents to the car, now came back to tug his sleeve. She turned to look at Cecily and frowned in consternation before whispering something to Marcus and tugging his sleeve again. At last he turned and followed her to the car.

As if she were released from a spell, Cecily snapped to attention. She shook her head to clear it, hopped into her truck, and drove away. She would go to the Henshaw's for a minute, and that was it.

But when she arrived, she couldn't get a moment alone with Marcus. She needed only a word to reassure herself about his condition, but his girlfriend sat steadily beside him and talked to the people who approached.

Marcus didn't say a word. He stared at the floor with the same intensity he had stared at Cecily. She sighed and headed for the kitchen. If she had to stay, she might as well make herself useful.

"What can I do?"

Libby Chapman Dobbins turned to her with a sad smile. "Hello, Cecily," she said kindly. The Chapmans were the nearest neighbors to the west. Libby and Mrs. Henshaw had always been close for some reason.

"How is Maggie?" Cecily asked. Maggie, Libby's younger sister, had been Mathew's girlfriend for the past two years and his best friend for most of their lives before that.

Libby's eyes filled with tears. "Not well, I'm afraid." Belatedly Cecily remembered that Libby and Marcus had dated before Libby's husband, Dobbie, came into the picture. She wondered how serious they had been and who broke it off.

"I'm sorry," Cecily said. "If there's anything I can do…" She trailed off. They both knew there was nothing she could do. While she had always been close to their other sister, Kitty, she hadn't had much contact with any of the other family.

"Thank you," Libby said. "Loaning us Dante is enough. He's been helpful with Maggie and Kitty as she tries to keep Maggie afloat."

Cecily nodded. Dante was her older brother and Kitty's boyfriend. He had been staying with the Chapmans since Mathew was killed a few days ago in order to offer whatever help and support he could.

"Here," Libby handed her a tray of appetizers. "If you wouldn't mind, you can pass this around and make sure everyone gets some. Times like these I think food is the only thing that can help." She smiled sadly again and turned her back to prepare another tray of food.

Cecily stared at the tray of food. It wasn't that she minded helping. The problem was that she looked dowdy and worn. The ranch was barely afloat, and she hadn't bought new clothes in two years. Her black dress and patent leather shoes had seen better days. Normally she wasn't insecure about her appearance because she stuck close to her ranch, but now she was in the home of the fabulously wealthy Henshaws, and she felt self-conscious. She straightened her spine and turned toward the living room. Certainly no one would pay attention to her clothes today of all days.

She circulated around the room and said a polite hello to friends and neighbors. When she reached Kitty and Dante they both gave her a one armed hug and kiss on the cheek.

"You look beautiful," Kitty whispered. She knew how self-conscious Cecily was about her lackluster wardrobe.

"Thanks," Cecily mouthed. Finally when everyone else in the room was served, she swallowed her fear and made her way to the couch.

"Would you like some food?" she asked. She was thankful her voice didn't tremor the way she feared it might.

"No thank you," the girlfriend said coolly. What was her name again? Laura? No, Lacey.

Marcus's head snapped up, but he didn't reach for the food.

"Marcus, eat something," she prompted gently.

He nodded and distractedly reached for an appetizer. She waited to make sure he took a bite before she turned to go back to the kitchen.

"Who is that girl?" Lacey asked, but Marcus didn't answer.

"Where is Maggie?" Cecily asked Libby when she returned to the kitchen.

"Dobbie and Dad took her home," Libby said. "It was too much for her."

Cecily nodded. The three older sisters seemed to be made of steel, but Maggie was fragile. She was all rainbows and sunshine, or she had been. Cecily hoped life wouldn't douse the roses in Maggie's cheeks. Hers were certainly gone. She squared her shoulders once again. Today wasn't about her or her problems.

She made the rounds with tray after tray of food Libby handed her, and each time she made sure Marcus ate. She didn't have to prompt him to do so anymore. He seemed to be watching for her. With every pass she made, the girlfriend became more uncomfortable.

"Who are you?" she blurted at last.

"I'm only a neighbor," Cecily said. "I live across the way. Mathew and I were the same age."

The girlfriend nodded, somewhat appeased. *Probably calculating the age difference and chalking me up as a harmless bystander,* Cecily thought. *Well, that's as good an assumption as any I could come up with.* She had yet to assign a name to the strange chemistry that now existed between her and Marcus.

Guests started to filter away. Mr. and Mrs. Henshaw retired to their bedroom upstairs. Libby remained to clean up the kitchen, and Cecily stayed to help her.

"What a sad day," Libby said.

"It is," Cecily agreed. "For both of your families. I know Maggie and Mathew were set to be married."

Libby nodded. Not many people knew of the engagement, but Kitty and Cecily were close. There were few secrets between them.

"Libby, why don't you go home to your husband? I can finish up here. You look all done in."

"Thanks, Cecily. I think I will." She surprised Cecily by hugging her tightly and kissing her cheek. "Take care."

"You, too," Cecily said.

When Libby left, Cecily returned her attention to the dishes. Lacey the Girlfriend's voice carried through from the living room, alerting Cecily to her continued presence. Was she staying all night? If so, how would Cecily ever get a moment alone with Marcus to make sure he was all right? The dishes were done at last and she could find no more reason to stay. She determined to forget her mission and leave. It was a crazy notion anyway; Marcus wasn't hers to check on. He had Lacey, and she had done an admirable job of standing by him all day.

As she reached for her purse she heard what she had been waiting for.

"Goodbye, Marcus. I'll call you tomorrow." There was the sound of a breezy kiss, and then the front door closed.

Cecily exited the kitchen. His back was to her, still sitting in the same position on the couch. She wondered if he had moved all day. She walked to him slowly and felt a wave of pain as she noted the sad slump of his shoulders. Marcus was one of those men who always knew what he was doing. He was supremely confident. To see him bent and broken was too much to bear.

He looked up as she approached and stood in front of him, and then he reached for her. Drawing her forward he pressed his head to her stomach and wrapped his arms tightly around her waist. And then he cried, great, heaving sobs she knew he hadn't released since learning of his brother's death.

At first she remained standing in front of him, smoothing her hand down his head over and over. She didn't talk; she merely held him and let him cry. After a while when it was clear there was no end in sight to his grief, she sat beside him on the couch, all without breaking contact with him. He remained firmly attached to her, shaking her body as his heaved with sobs.

He held her so tightly she had trouble breathing, but she didn't complain or try to move away. For whatever reason she had been elected to provide him comfort. She had no right to balk at the opportunity. He needed her, and she would help him.

Eventually his weeping subsided into soft crying, and then he was quiet. She chanced looking down at his face and found he was asleep. She smiled. He looked peaceful in sleep, like a sweet little boy. She eased out of his embrace, noting as she did that her dress was soaked with his tears. He didn't stir. She wondered when he had last slept. She peeled off his boots, tucked his feet up on the couch, and covered him with a blanket. She kissed him softly on the forehead and walked to the edge of the room to retrieve her keys. She paused in the entryway and looked back. As she did she had the strange sense her life had just changed forever.

CHAPTER 2

$\mathcal{L}$ife returned to normal for Cecily. She chalked her odd premonition up to the emotion of the day and tried to forget all about Marcus Henshaw. She didn't succeed completely, but she was able to block him from her mind enough to function at a normal level.

And then Sunday rolled around. Marcus had stopped attending their church years ago, so Cecily had no fears about running into him there—until she physically ran into him as soon as she entered the building.

"Oh," she said. She had been reading her bulletin as she entered the sanctuary when she walked into a burly form she looked up to apologize, but the words died on her lips.

Marcus grasped her upper arms to keep her from falling, and his fingers curled softly around her biceps. "Okay?"

She nodded. He had nice eyes, she thought. "Are you?" Her words held a deeper meaning, and he knew it.

He nodded. "Thanks." She heard what he left unspoken, too. *Thanks for being there. Thanks for staying. Thanks for comforting me.*

She nodded. Unbidden, her gaze dropped to his lips, and she watched them curve into a smile.

Music started and she jumped slightly. What was she doing? This was church—her tiny church where people talked and doted on the slightest nuance. Here she was having a tête-à-tête with Montana's version of *The Bachelor*. She dropped her gaze and pivoted out of his grasp, finding her seat in her regular pew.

Bad timing. That was the story of her life. If she and Marcus had discovered their strange attraction to each other a few years ago, she would have jumped at the opportunity and pursued him. She had once been a fun and carefree girl who thought life couldn't possibly ever deal her a bad hand. She had also been the biggest flirt this side of the Mississippi, and probably east of it, too. Previously if she ever thought she stood a chance with Marcus, she would have done anything to capture his interest and attention. And then her world turned upside down.

Her beloved father, the closest person on earth to her, had become involved with a militant militia. With them he kidnapped a state senator. Her brother, Dante, had worked as an informant for the FBI. He begged for leniency for their father, but he still received a penalty of ten years in federal prison. On top of that, his legal bills had almost bankrupted them. Dante was in college at the time. He had offered to drop out and run the ranch, but their mother wouldn't hear of it. Their parents were divorced and their mother lived in Chicago. Despite the divorce, Cecily's father and mother were very much in love and had rekindled their relationship after his arrest. She sent money when she could, and it helped some, but the brunt of responsibility fell on Cecily's shoulders.

For the first couple of years she had floundered. Despite the fact that she had lived on the ranch her whole life, she knew nothing about cows. Her father and their ranch hands had done all the work, and she had reaped the rewards—such as her pretty horse. She delighted in him and used him as an escape from the stress of her new life. And then one day she was out riding and it hit her. *Horses*. She might not know one end of a cow from another, but horses were almost her obsession. She had land. She had barns. Why not trade her cows for horses? All the ranchers in the area used horses, but there wasn't a horse ranch for miles. Whenever a rancher in the area needed a new horse he had to drive for hours to get one. If she started a quality breeding program, she could not only serve the ranchers in the area, but in other areas, too.

It was a long, arduous process still only in its fledgling stages. She had barely begun to show a profit and probably wouldn't for a couple of years, but she knew she would succeed because she was passionate. She loved her horses; she loved her new business. Perhaps she loved it even more because it was her own. This wasn't a business she had been handed; it was one she had started from scratch, and its success or failure depended on her. Her shoulders straightened thinking about it. There was no room for failure. She would succeed or die trying, and she was determined to succeed.

The problem was that she hadn't told her father what she was up to. She didn't want to face the possibility of his wrath when he found out she was dismantling the business his grandfather had started in order to raise horses, something he'd had very little time for or interest in. Still, she doggedly pressed on. Her father wasn't here; she was. She had to do what was best, so she worked from sun up to sun down every day of the week but Sunday when she took a day off to attend church.

When her pastor announced it was time to stand and greet one another she realized she hadn't been paying attention for most of the service already. She smiled at the little old lady next to her and shook her hand. Then she turned to the seat behind her and froze. Marcus was there with his mother and father. He smiled at her and held out his hand. She gave him a tentative smile and placed her hand in his. When their palms touched she realized he was pressing a slip of folded paper into her hand. She pressed her thumb to it and withdrew her hand.

She sat and made herself wait until the prayer before the offering to open the paper.

"Have lunch with me. Mill's Park. I'll bring the food."

She had to read it three times to make sure she understood it correctly. There was no question, only a command.

If he thinks he can order me around like a servant, he has another think coming, she thought. She vowed she wouldn't go and silently listed all the reasons for her refusal in her head. But when the service was over and Marcus looked at her with one eyebrow arched in question, she gave a slight nod and turned her head away to hide her grimace. *Spineless coward,* she accused herself. Or maybe she was curious. After all, it could be possible he wanted to talk business. Maybe he had heard of her new horse venture somehow. She had been keeping it under her hat, but things had a way of leaking out in their small community. She shuddered. If there was one thing she didn't want leaked, it was her meeting with Marcus. She could only imagine how that would go over. *Poor Cecily Blake is chasing Marcus Henshaw. She's pretty, but can you imagine the nerve? He could have any woman he wants, and she's six years too young for him. They say his girlfriend was a runner up for Miss Montana...*

She knew how the gossip would go because she had heard it all before. Once upon a time she had even participated in it, but that was then; this was now. Now she kept to herself and didn't gossip about her neighbors; now she knew how much gossip hurt.

There's the Blake girl. Her father's in prison. I wonder how she'll turn out. You know what they say about apples and trees. She had actually heard someone say that about her once. She had pressed her lips together to stop their trembling and turned her head to hide her tears. She had understood then what everyone else already knew: she was tainted by her father's crime. Everyone seemed to forget the good Yancey Blake had done for the community. Instead they chose to dwell on his one glaring sin, and she was condemned along with him.

The church service ended, and she was ashamed to realize she hadn't heard one word of the sermon. She couldn't even be certain she had sung the closing hymn. Instead her mind had been performing mental gymnastics as she pondered what Marcus could possibly want with her. Whatever it was, it couldn't be worse than the uncertainty of not knowing.

CHAPTER 3

*C*ecily took her time driving to the one and only park in their small town, but she still beat him there. She used the time to scout an out of the way spot where they could remain undetected. Finally she found it and hoped he would be able to locate her truck in the remote setting she had selected. Only when she saw his truck pull in did she realize how it might look to him—as if she had selected a hidden spot in order to have an uninterrupted rendezvous with him.

"I didn't choose this spot for its makeout potential," she blurted as soon as he approached her truck.

He laughed and opened her door.

"I mean, I thought it would be more private back here. Away from prying eyes."

He nodded, but still didn't speak. Instead he set aside the bag of takeout food he was holding and put up his arms to lift her down.

She realized when he touched her it was a mistake to let him do so. A thrill of electricity shot from her ribs where his fingers were pressed to the rest of her body, all the way to her fingers and toes. She wondered if he felt it, too, because he paused with her body suspended in midair and looked at her. He finally set her down and picked up the food. He turned away and headed to the shade of a giant oak tree.

What is wrong with you? Get hold of yourself, she commanded. She swallowed hard and smoothed down her flyaway hair. She could do this. She was no stranger to dating. While in Chicago with her mother, she had dated a couple dozen different men and kept them all chasing her.

"You're a man of few words, huh, Marcus?" she said.

He threw her a smile over his shoulder but remained mute.

"Or is this some long, complicated version of charades? *Walking Tall,*" she guessed. "No, *Silence is Golden,*" she tried again.

"How about 'stop chattering, Cecily, we've reached our destination,'" he said. He sat and began to set out containers of food. "Are you always this chatty?"

"Don't you know?" she asked. "You've known me all my life." She smiled and batted her long lashes at him. That had worked with more than one guy. More than a few of them had commented on her long and pretty lashes.

"There's knowing someone, and then there's *knowing* someone." He leaned toward her. "I know you, but I don't really *know* you." His voice was low and intimate. A shiver worked its way up her spine, but she refused to acknowledge it.

She leaned forward so they were a mere two inches apart. "Did you hone these flirting skills at college? If so, maybe I'll give higher education another thought."

"You're a bad kid."

She grinned. "Not anymore. I've reformed."

"Why?" He handed her a sandwich. "Being bad is so much fun."

"Being bad is a luxury I can't afford. I have a ranch to run."

He smiled. "Now *that* I understand. I think I've been a grownup since I was ten."

She considered him as she nibbled her sandwich. She always assumed he had it all: wealth, power, good looks. It never occurred to her how hard he worked to get it, or that he had taken over responsibility for his ranch at such a young age.

"Then let's be kids again, if only for today. What do you want to do?"

"Make out with a pretty girl," he said.

Her cheeks flamed. "Pick something else."

He smiled. "Spoilsport. Hmm." He chewed and looked around the park. "Let's wade in the creek."

"Sounds fun," she said, and she smiled, too. "I haven't done that since I was a kid."

"You're still a kid."

"Thanks for the reminder, Pops. I meant when I was a little kid."

"Did you play outdoors a lot?"

"Yes, but I preferred to play house or babies or something girly. Kitty and Dante always wanted to read or search for leaves to press or boring stuff like that."

"They seem happy together."

She nodded. "Now that he's graduated I don't think it will be long before they're engaged."

"What about you, do you have a boyfriend?" It wasn't her imagination his tone turned crisp.

"Several," she said and smiled unrepentantly when he narrowed his eyes at her. She finished her meal and put her head back to soak up the sunshine. "What a glorious day." She sensed his eyes on her. When she opened her eyes to look at him, he was watching her with the intensity she had come to recognize. She wondered what he was thinking when he looked at her that way.

"Come here," he commanded. He took her hand and pulled her toward him so she was almost touching him. His hand rose to touch her hair haltingly, reverently. "Don't ever cut your hair," he said. "It's beautiful. You look exotic."

She wanted to say something flippant and funny, but words failed her as her heartbeat stuck in her throat and cut off any chance of a reply. Marcus was intimidating, and Cecily had never been intimidated by a man before.

"Cecily," he whispered, touching his fingertips softly to her lips.

Against her will they opened and she kissed his fingertips. His hand slid to her cheek and cupped it. She could feel herself being drawn in to his embrace.

"Marcus," she whispered.

He opened his eyes slightly to look at her.

"Catch me," she said. Before he could react she jumped to her feet and darted away.

It took him a moment to realize what had happened, but when he did, he stood and took off after her. She was athletic and fast, and she had a head start, so she beat him to the stream, threw off her shoes, and plunged into the water. It was cold, and the shock worked to clear any vestiges of attraction that still lingered. She had to be careful. Marcus was not a man she could play games with and hope to win. She could not, would not kiss him again. Not when everything was uncertain and topsy-turvy. Not when she was poor as a field mouse and he had a serious girlfriend. Not when he was still mourning his brother. Not when she couldn't understand the strange power he had over her; the list went on and on.

He sat on the streambed to remove his boots. "You're a tease, Cecily Blake," he said, but there was faint amusement in his tone.

"I'm twenty," she pointed out. "I'm supposed to be a tease, and I don't have the luxury of your many years of experience."

"You are asking for it, aren't you?" He pulled off his socks and stuffed them in his boots.

"No, I'm not," she said seriously. "We're here to have fun and that's all."

He grinned. "There are many different kinds of fun."

"And you've no doubt experienced them all."

"Jealous?"

"No, I'm happy for you. When I'm old I want fond memories to look back on, too."

He stood and put his hands on his hips. "Come here so I may punish you."

"Come and get me, but be careful on the rocks. I don't want you to fall and break a hip. That can be dangerous for someone your age."

He kept his gaze focused on her as he stepped into the water. "You must really want to be caught if you're not running away," he said.

Her smile widened. "Keep the dream alive, Marcus."

He reached out his arms to her and then, a second before he reached her, he pitched forward and down. His arms windmilled wildly, looking for a handhold.

"Oh, I forgot to tell you there's a drop off there, and it's a few feet deep," she said. She grinned as she peered down at him. He was almost waist deep in water after his fall.

He wiped his face and shook water droplets off his hair. "Better run little girl, because when I get hold of you, you're going to get it."

"What am I going to get?" she asked.

"Stay there and I'll show you." He pulled himself out of his hole, but she was already sprinting away as best she could on the slippery rocks.

He splashed along behind her, clumsy and oafish with his big feet and wet denim. "Are you part mermaid?" he asked. "How are you maneuvering these rocks so easily?"

In response she giggled. He smiled. Her laughter was endearing. He had heard her laugh many times over the years and never thought anything of it, but now he couldn't remember the last time she had laughed. His last few glimpses of her had been a study in sadness; life had turned hard for Cecily, and Marcus had the sudden urge to make it better.

When he was about to reach her she screamed and threw herself into his arms.

"What? What is it?" he asked.

"Snake," she said. She pressed her face to his neck. He looked behind her and saw the tail of a snake disappear into the water.

"It's gone," he said. Unconsciously his hand smoothed down her back.

She pulled her head back from his neck. He wished she would put it back. He liked the feel of her cradled against him.

"It was real," she said defensively. "There really was a snake."

"I know," he soothed. "I saw it."

She relaxed.

"Why are you so tense?"

She swallowed hard and looked away from him. "I don't want you to think I'm chasing you."

He threw back his head and laughed. She tried to pull away but he pinned her to him. "Chasing me? Cecily, you haven't spoken one solitary word to me in two long years. *I* invited *you* today, remember? I'm fairly certain I would be thrilled if I thought you were chasing me."

"Why? Why did you invite me?" Her hands seemed to be out of her control as they smoothed along his chest and biceps.

He kept his left hand on her waist, but his right hand slid up to tangle in her mass of dark hair. "I haven't been able to stop thinking of you one day the last two years. You obsess me."

She was startled by the admission and her face showed it. He leaned in to kiss her, but she held up a hand and pressed it to his lips. "No."

"Why?"

"You know why. There's an impossible gulf between us."

"One kiss," he begged. "Please, please put me out of my misery and give me one kiss. I have to know if it was a fluke."

She was curious about that, too. Had that explosive kiss between them been some sort of error? Was it because he saved her life their passion flared to such heights so quickly?

"All right," she agreed softly. "One kiss."

Her arms slid up and around him so her hands rested on the base of his skull. He used the hand in her hair to position her head at a slight angle, and then he kissed her. And then it happened. Cecily closed her eyes and everything went black, and then a brilliant white as something dazzling exploded behind her eyes. She couldn't hear, she couldn't see, but she could feel, and what she felt was Marcus. Marcus touching her waist, his hand in her hair and drawing her closer, Marcus's lips pressed to hers.

One of them was trembling, but they were so enmeshed in each other Cecily didn't know which one it was. Maybe it was both of them. All she knew was she was utterly incapable of pulling away from him, and he must have felt the same because the kiss went on, and on, and on.

CHAPTER 4

*A*t last Cecily's toes were becoming numb from the coolness of the stream. Reluctantly she pulled away from him and his lips followed, clinging to hers, willing her not to break the moment. Finally they rested their foreheads together and sucked air as they tried to return their breathing to normal.

"What was that?" Marcus asked. His voice was shaky.

"I wish I knew," Cecily said. She could barely get the words out. She was trembling.

"You're cold," he said.

"Am I?" She didn't feel cold. She felt…she wasn't sure what she felt, but it was something she had never experienced before.

He bent and swept her into his arms, carried her out of the stream, and set her down on the bank. They stood toe to toe looking at each other, not touching and not speaking. He reached up to tuck a strand of hair behind her ear, and her whole body was electrified from the brief contact.

"Our shoes are down there," she said. She pointed a dozen feet downstream

He nodded.

Neither of them made a move for a few more seconds. Then he

placed his hand on her waist and she jumped. He started to lean toward her again, but she moved away.

"Marcus, no. We said one kiss."

"Things change," he said.

"Not between us they don't. Or have you suddenly broken up with Miss Montana?"

He gave a reluctant smile at her jealous tone. "No, Lacey and I are still together."

She nodded, frowning. Not only had she kissed Marcus, but she had broken her own rules and kissed someone who had a girlfriend. "Let's find our shoes." She moved away from him and his hand dropped listlessly to his side.

They refastened their shoes and walked side by side back to their vehicles.

"Thank you for lunch," she said politely. She opened her truck door and turned to face him. He surprised her by brushing his knuckles gently along her jaw.

"Doesn't anyone ever call you anything besides Cecily?"

"No."

"I'm going to," he said. He grasped her waist and lifted her carefully into her seat. "This isn't over." He took her hand and kissed the back of it. "See you later, Lee."

She didn't move a muscle until she saw him hop up into his truck cab, start it up, and drive away. She turned to face forward and closed her door.

"He called me Lee," she said dumbly, and then she rested her head on the steering wheel and cried. The raw passion between them had left her dazed and frazzled, breaking open the tight container she had built around her emotions. It was a long time later that she returned to her ranch, weak and exhausted.

From that day forward, Marcus came to church every Sunday. And every Sunday he asked her to the park. And every time he asked Cecily refused.

She held her breath to see if news of their meeting had leaked, but it hadn't. She was realistic enough to know that while they might be able to get away with one clandestine encounter their secret wouldn't keep on a weekly basis. Besides that, she was downright afraid of him. One touch, one look and she would give in to him, to his kisses. She wasn't so naïve she didn't realize where their level of kissing would lead if they kept it up, and that was a can of worms she wasn't willing to open.

Besides church she ran into him once in the store.

"Don't tell me you do the shopping for your family, too," she said. Seeing him on a weekly basis while trying to avoid him was making her nervous and irritable.

He smiled. "I'm picking up something for my mom." His fingers brushed her waist. "Have lunch with me."

She shook her head.

"Chicken," he whispered.

"Bock, bock," she replied.

His laughter echoed behind her as she almost sprinted away from him.

Finally it was July fourth. She wasn't sure if his family would hold their annual celebration, but they must have decided to go on with life as usual because his mother called to invite her and all her ranch hands.

Cecily had to repress a smile as she accepted the invitation. If Mrs. Henshaw knew how few hands the Blakes had now, she would plan for less food. Then she realized she probably should tell her so she would do so.

"Mrs. Henshaw, we only have a handful of help coming this year. Also, my brother has a friend in from out of town that week. Would it be an imposition if he tagged along?"

"Certainly not, dear. You bring anyone you like."

"Thank you, ma'am," Cecily said. She had always liked Mrs. Henshaw; she was a sweet woman.

"As far as food goes your cook knows what to do. She sends the same thing every year."

Cecily's pride wouldn't allow her to tell the older woman they'd let their cook go. It must be a sign of how much the Henshaws had withdrawn from society if she didn't know.

"Would you remind me, please, what she brings? I'm afraid I can't remember."

"A fruit salad."

"That's all?" Cecily asked. "Surely we can contribute more than that." She had never realized how paltry their offering was in comparison to everyone else. Mrs. Henshaw cooked enough beef to make up an entire cow, and Libby Dobbins made almost everything else.

"You may bring whatever you'd like, dear. Thank you for asking." She sounded pleasantly surprised by Cecily's offer.

"I'll do that. See you in a few days, Mrs. Henshaw. Thank you."

"You're welcome, dear. Take care."

"You, too."

She hung up thinking what a nice woman Mrs. Henshaw was. Marcus was more reserved with his emotions, like his father. Mathew had received his mother's outright sweetness.

What would she be like as a mother-in-law, Cecily wondered, and then blushed at the unbidden thought and sent it away. *I'm sure one day soon Lacey-the-Beautiful will find out.* Her teeth slammed together with force and then ground into each other. Lacey was walking perfection from the tip of her lustrous hair to the soles of her beautiful feet. And her feet were beautiful; Cecily had checked. She was obviously Marcus's type. She fit the image of their wealthy perfection in a way Cecily never could. Even though she loved pretty things, running her own business had turned her into a rough and tumble cowgirl.

She hated the man-obsessed woman she was turning into, and resenting Marcus for making her think of him so often. It was an irrational anger, but it gave her solace from her other more complicated emotions and desires, so she held onto it.

It shouldn't have come as a surprise when Marcus showed up one Monday morning as she stood watching her new stallion run in the corral.

"That's a fine looking specimen," he said. He came up to stand beside her and she was reminded of that day two years ago when they had shared their first fateful kiss.

She feigned surprise as she turned to look at him, but of course she had been intensely aware of him since his truck entered their long lane.

"Thank you, he's a recent purchase."

"I wasn't talking about the horse, but he looks nice, too." He looked around. "I see more horses than cows."

"Have you come to spy on me?"

"We Henshaws like to keep an eye on the competition."

The thought of their tiny ranch being competition for the Henshaw's vast spread was laughable, and so she laughed. "What do you want, really?"

"You know what I want," he said. His tone was low and intimate. He didn't touch her, but she reacted as if he did by leaning more of her weight on the fence for support. She swallowed and found her throat suddenly dry. "You've been avoiding me."

"True enough," she said.

"Why?"

"You know why."

He let out a frustrated breath. "It won't work, Lee, not with the way things are between us."

"The way things are between us," she echoed. "You mean how you have a girlfriend and we're from two different worlds?"

Now it was his turn to echo her. "Two different worlds? What are you talking about? We've been neighbors for generations."

"And that's as close as we'll ever get socially."

"Oh, for heaven's sake. Grow up, little girl. This isn't the eighteenth century. Wealth means nothing in the scheme of things."

"You can only say that when you're the one who is wealthy," she told him. She noticed he didn't address the issue of his girlfriend as an obstacle between them.

"You're being difficult," he said.

"I'm being impossible, which is in keeping with our current circumstances. I won't be what you want me to be, Marcus."

"How do you know what I want you to be?" he asked.

"Because I know," she said. He wanted to maintain his current girlfriend and keep her, Cecily, as a side dish. Only she wouldn't comply, and it was making him angry. "I may not have much, but I have my pride and my reputation. I intend to keep both in tact."

Instead of making him angry her words amused him. He gave her a cocky half smile she found annoyingly endearing. "You can run, Lee, but you can't hide." He placed a hand on either side of the rail behind her so she was pinned to the fence and pressed close against him. "I know where you live and also where you work."

"You have no idea how stubborn I can be," she told him. It was an effort to get the words out. The proximity of his body, so close to hers, was having its usual numbing effect on her brain.

"I intend to find out," he said. His gaze dropped to her lips, but he didn't try to kiss her. He lingered a half inch away, and then he let go of the fence and strode away.

She remained leaning against the fencepost for support until she could no longer see his vehicle in the long driveway, and then she sagged to the ground and rested her head on her knees.

Blast you, Marcus Henshaw, she thought as she sucked in an unsteady breath. He had no right to show up here and throw her off balance. Her home was her sanctuary, the one place she was safe and free to let down her guard. Now that safety was gone. From now on every truck she heard would cause her heart to pound, wondering if it might be him, and halfway hoping it was.

You won't win, she raged inwardly. *You can try, but you won't. I've lost my family name, my youth, and any future outside of this ranch, but you won't win my pride or my integrity.*

But even as she thought it her fingers pressed against her lips as she remembered the way he had kissed her a few weeks ago in the stream.

She let out a groan and dropped her head to her knees once more. She would keep him at bay; she had to, or she would lose herself completely.

CHAPTER 5

Thankfully a distraction arrived in time for the fourth of July.

Radley Winston was her brother's college roommate, and he was as unusual as his name. Though Dante had only lived on campus a year, their friendship had survived, and they were close. When Radley met Cecily, they had formed an instant friendship that lasted, too, despite the fact that they rarely saw each other. Since graduating Radley had started his own computer company that was already causing buzz on Wall Street. He was cute, sweet, and slightly geeky, much like Dante. And he had a not so secret crush on Cecily.

He was too shy to admit his feelings, so they shared a light and innocent flirtation. Cecily dated other people, but she always kept Radley in the back of her mind. Someday, when she was ready to settle down, he was the type of guy she wanted; intelligent, kind, and good. The sort of guy who would make an excellent husband and father.

Now she found herself nervous as the day of Radley's arrival approached. What if he had found someone else? She had no claim on him, after all. It would be a blow to have her backup move on when she needed him most.

She needn't have worried, though. As soon as Kitty and Dante pulled up with him after picking him up from town, he sprang up the steps, threw open the door to the house, picked Cecily up and twirled her in a dizzying circle.

"Did you miss me?" he asked.

"I did," she said sincerely. He was a sweetheart, and she liked him very much. She kissed his cheek and hugged his neck, enjoying the faint blush that tinged his cheeks.

He set her down and they inspected each other.

"You look older," she said.

"And you look prettier. I think ranch life agrees with you."

She thought it agreed with her, too. She had never been happier or more fulfilled. She finally found her purpose. The feeling of being in control of her destiny was a heady one, if at times lonely.

"What are we going to do tonight?" This came from Dante. He stood in the doorway with his arm around Kitty. Kitty was asking Cecily questions with her eyes, and Cecily was attempting to answer. *Did she have feelings for Radley? If so, what were they?* Finally she gave a slight shrug to her best friend. She would have to figure out later how she felt about him. He was staying for an entire week.

Cecily felt some measure of guilt when she was around Kitty now. She hadn't told her anything about Marcus, and it was the only secret she had ever kept. Her guilt eased when she remembered Kitty had kept her relationship with Dante a secret in the beginning. Now she understood why. Some things were too puzzling and private to share with anyone, even someone you loved like a sister.

"I'll cook," she suggested. "And then we can go for a ride. Radley has been away from horses too long." She pinched his side.

He put an arm around her and pulled her close. "You're going to cook for me, Cecily? You know this means we're married in some cultures."

"Better wait until you've tasted it," she said. "You might ask for a divorce."

"Never," he said, and something flashed in his eyes that made her look away.

"Cecily is an amazing cook," Kitty volunteered. "I had no idea until recently."

Cecily smiled. "Neither did I. I never had to do it before, but now that we let Marla go someone has to keep us fed." Cooking was one more thing she had started reluctantly and then realized she had a talent for. *Maybe it's a good thing my life got flipped upside down*, she thought. *I'm finding out there's more to me than I ever would have guessed.*

One of their few remaining ranch hands, a cowboy who had been with them forever, was an avid gardener. Cecily never appreciated that fact until she started to cook. Now she relished the bounty he created. For supper she served corn on the cob, tomato pie, and grilled steaks.

"Do you ever get tired of having steak?" Radley asked. Beef was plentiful in the middle of cattle country.

"No," Kitty, Cecily, and Dante answered in unison.

"I don't think I would, either," Radley said. He gave Cecily a purposeful look, but she wasn't sure what he was trying to tell her.

After supper they saddled the horses and went for a ride.

"I want to see the shack where you guys were held," Radley said. When Cecily's father and the militia kidnapped the state senator, Dante and Kitty got in the way. They were also tied up and held in a shack in the woods.

"It's on the Henshaw's property," Cecily said warily.

"The edge of their property," Dante said. "They won't care. They won't even know."

That was probably true. The Henshaws owned almost fifty thousand acres. Until the kidnapping they didn't even remember the shack. Besides, it wasn't as if she was going to run into Marcus in the middle of the woods.

"All right," she said reluctantly.

Kitty, ever observant, was frowning at her. "Is everything all right, Cecily? You're not feuding with the Henshaws, are you?"

Cecily laughed, but it sounded brittle. "Of course not. Everything is fine." She smoothed a hand over her flyaway hair and tucked it into a ponytail at the base of her neck.

Kitty kept up her worried stare until Cecily urged her horse forward and took the lead.

"Wow, sis, your sense of direction is getting almost as good as Dad's," Dante said.

"I had to learn these woods really well when the reporters and tourists were here," she said. After the kidnapping their community became famous and people poured in from all over to see where the big event took place. "More than a few of them got lost."

"I'm glad the notoriety has died down," Kitty said.

"Me, too. I was worried it would start up again with Mathew's death, but so far everything seems calm." Mathew had been killed by one of the Henshaw's ranch hands who had an obsession with Maggie. After the murder he ran and hadn't been seen since, although he threatened Maggie and she had to be sent away for her safety.

A pall settled over the group at the mention of Mathew's death.

"There." Cecily broke the silence and pointed to the little shack some distance ahead of them.

"I'm surprised the Henshaws didn't tear it down when all the tourists started pouring in," Kitty said.

"I think they preferred to pretend nothing was happening. That seems to be their way—to keep going no matter what and live above it all," Dante said.

"Let's see inside it," Radley said.

Cecily dismounted and held his reins so he could get down.

"Thanks," he said. "Someday I'll get the hang of it."

"You're getting better," she said.

"I had nowhere to go but up." They shared a smile. His first time on a horse hadn't gone well after it took off while he only had one leg in the saddle. He was dragged for a few feet before her father rescued him. She was surprised and impressed he tried again after that.

He took her hand as they headed to the shack, and she had to hide her surprise. Besides a hug goodbye or hello and a few pecks on the cheek they didn't usually touch.

"This is it," Dante said as they stood in the entrance to the shack.

"This is where I learned my girl is a real live action hero." He put his arm around Kitty's waist and kissed her cheek.

"Dante," Kitty said shyly. When they were kidnapped, she had been carrying a knife and a gun, and she was able to rescue him and his father. Cecily was still in awe of her bravery and resourcefulness. If she didn't love her before, she would love her now for saving her father and brother.

"Why don't you reenact for us, Kitty, how you roundhouse kicked all the bad guys and then used a bullwhip to subdue them," Radley said.

"That's not what happened," Kitty said.

"That's how Dante tells it," Radley said. He winked at Cecily.

"I may have embellished slightly," Dante agreed.

"You're naughty, Dante," Kitty said.

"I'm an actuary. We get that a lot." He pinched Kitty's waist and she giggled again. She was extremely ticklish.

Behind them a tree branch snapped and a horse whinnied. Cecily turned to look with a sinking heart. Instinct told her who it would be, and she was correct. Marcus sat atop his stallion with his rifle slung over his back.

"I thought I saw someone enter these woods," he said. "I thought it might be tourists again." His tone was friendly until his eyes settled on Cecily's hand where it was joined to Radley. His eyes narrowed, but his gaze didn't waiver.

"I'm sorry, Marcus," Dante said. "We should have called for permission. My college roommate is in town, and he wanted the play by play on our little adventure." He smiled. Marcus didn't.

"No problem," he said, although his tone was less than friendly now.

An awkward silence settled over the group.

"Is your mother doing all right with the July fourth preparations?" Kitty asked. "I'll help in any way I can."

"She likes to keep busy," Marcus said distractedly. "Thank you all the same." His eyes finally moved from Cecily's hand. They settled on Radley's face. "I didn't catch your name."

"I'm sorry," Dante said. "My manners are all over the place today. This is Radley Winston, my good friend."

Marcus nodded. "I'm Marcus Henshaw. Welcome to Montana."

Cecily wondered if anyone else heard the challenge in his tone. "Good day," he added. He tipped his hat to them, then turned his horse and headed for home.

The group watched him go in silence and waited to speak until he was out of sight.

"Was that a Montana greeting, or was that weird?" Radley asked.

"No, that was weird," Dante said. "I don't know him well, but that seemed out of character."

"Maybe it's the grief," Kitty suggested. "It changes people."

The three of them looked at Cecily as if waiting for her to weigh in with an opinion. "Maybe he's weird." She smiled to herself as she imagined what Marcus would say if he heard her. Most likely he wouldn't *say* anything. He would chase her and then kiss her and then…

She broke off because she was smiling like an idiot and clasping Radley's hand to her chin.

"Um," she said. She dropped their hands to her side once again. "Let's go back. I'll see what I can scrounge for dessert.

"I have some ideas," Radley said, softly so only she could hear him. He winked at her and smiled.

"Interesting," she said. It was the best word to describe her life right now. Very, very interesting.

CHAPTER 6

The next few days flew by in a blur and then it was July fourth. Cecily was having a nice time with Radley, although she didn't get to spend as much time with him as she would like. She was busy with the ranch from sunup until sundown. At first he followed her around and tried to help out, but then he realized he was getting in her way more than he was helping, so he stuck with Kitty and Dante and waited for her to come back to the house at night.

She learned he could cook, too, and was treated to a few meals by him. As much as she loved to cook, it was nice to come in from a long day of hard work and find supper waiting for her.

"This is how a man must feel," she blurted one night. She worried she might have offended him, but he laughed.

"I wouldn't know. You're the only girl who has ever cooked for me, but it was nice." He looked like he was going to lean in for a kiss but Kitty and Dante entered the room.

"For a remote ranch in the middle of nowhere there isn't much privacy," he whispered.

Cecily laughed, but a part of her was relieved. She liked Radley, really liked him, but she wasn't sure she was attracted to him. Maybe when she finally did give in and kiss him she would experience the same fireworks she had with Marcus.

Her heart picked up its pace. That would be a dream come true, to find passion with Radley when they had so many other things going for them. They were on the same level and, most of all, he was available. She didn't have to contend with a beauty pageant girlfriend and millions of dollars in his case.

"I'm not at all sure I want to go to the Fourth of July celebration," Radley said as they made their way to the Henshaw's ranch. "That guy we met looked like he wanted to drive me out to the middle of nowhere and leave me for dead."

"He's harmless. He was probably having a bad day. Besides, he's lots older than us and doesn't hang around with us. He stays with the men or with his girlfriend," Kitty said.

Cecily looked out the window. Would perfect Lacey be there today?

The answer was yes. She greeted everyone like she was queen of the castle, a fact which Cecily found supremely annoying.

They're not even engaged, but she acts like she owns him and the ranch.

Her heart plummeted as a new thought occurred to her. Were they engaged? Had she somehow missed that? Was Marcus secretly pursuing her because he was panicking over his engagement? Surreptitiously she checked Lacey's hand for a ring. Her heart relaxed when she didn't see one. Maybe it was being sized. She shook her head. She was being ridiculous. Even if they were engaged it was no business of hers.

"Are you all right, love?" Radley asked. He laid a gentle hand on her back. She was as surprised at his touch as she was by his endearment.

"I'm fine," she said. To her right Marcus cleared his throat. She turned to look at him and he shook his head slightly. What did that mean? It was almost like he was telling her to move away from Radley's touch. If so, he would have a long wait until she complied. She tipped her head up and tucked her arm into Radley's elbow.

"Let's sit," she suggested.

"Sure," he agreed. He led her to a straw bale and they sat side by side.

"That's a lot of food." Radley nodded his head toward the long food table. "Who's that girl?"

"That's Libby. She's Kitty's sister. She's an awesome cook. She and Mrs. Henshaw prepare most of the food."

"I think you're an awesome cook, and you provided a lot, too," he said proudly. He took her hand and twined their fingers together. "How far along is she?"

"What?" she asked. She turned her attention from the food table to him.

He nodded his head toward Libby again. "The girl, Libby, she's pregnant. How far along is she?"

Cecily's mouth fell in surprise. She looked at Libby and her shock deepened. Indeed, her stomach was slightly rounded and she looked fatigued and green around the gills. "I had no idea she was expecting. How did you know?"

"My sister is pregnant with her first. Libby looks the same, like she's uncomfortable and about to fall asleep standing up."

She shook her head, wondering why Kitty hadn't told her. Maybe Libby wasn't announcing it publicly yet. Although after today that was going to be a moot point. Now that she was paying attention her condition was obvious, especially when her husband, Dobbie, came over to check on her and then laid a gentle hand on her stomach when he leaned in to kiss her cheek.

"She's young to have a baby," Radley said.

"She's twenty two," Cecily said. "That's a normal age here."

"That's very young in Chicago, almost still a teenager. People don't start having kids until their thirties where I'm from." He paused. "Do you want kids young?"

The question caught her off guard. Did she? She had honestly never thought about it, which was strange considering how much she used to love to play house. "I think I want to wait a while, at least until I get the new business up and running. Oh, and I have to fall in love and get married first." She grinned at him.

"If there's anything I can do to help you out, let me know. With any part of that." He wagged his eyebrows at her.

"Radley, I think you've changed."

"I've grown up, I guess, and become more aggressive about getting what I want."

She flushed and looked away, suddenly flustered. He knew what he wanted, but did she? Unbidden, her eyes sought Marcus as he stood across the room. Like usual he was staring at her. He shook his head at her again. Her flush deepened and she looked away. What did that mean? Why did he keep shaking his head at her?

"Let's eat," Mr. Henshaw boomed. He asked the blessing for the food and the line formed. To her consternation Marcus positioned himself behind her and Radley, and she was sure it was on purpose.

"How long have you two been together?" He ignored Cecily and asked Radley the question.

"Uh, we've known each other three years," Radley said uncomfortably, and no wonder. Marcus was asking about something they'd never discussed or put a name to.

"And have you been together all that time?" Marcus continued.

"Uh," Radley said.

"Where's your girlfriend?" Cecily asked. She turned to Radley. "Did you know Mr. Henshaw's girlfriend was a runner up in the Miss Montana pageant?" She squinted as she pretended to think. "Which year was that? My childhood memories are foggy, but I remember watching that pageant right before I watched cartoons."

Marcus smiled. "I have it on DVD. I would be glad to show it to you in order to jog your memory. Let me know when I can bring it over, or I could stop by."

"Sorry, but I'm much too busy for visitors," Cecily said.

Marcus's smile widened. "Sorry to hear that." He turned to Radley. "You must be lonely having to entertain yourself."

"Radley isn't a visitor, he's like family," Cecily snapped.

"Like your brother I would guess," Marcus said.

Radley frowned, vaguely aware he'd been insulted, but not sure how.

"Sleep tight with that thought," Cecily said sweetly.

Marcus frowned. He opened his mouth to say more but they reached the head of the line. She handed Radley a plate and took one of her own.

"Hello, Libby," Marcus said softly, sweetly. "How are you doing?"

"I'm fine, Marcus. How are you?" Her question went beyond the surface.

"Hanging in there," Marcus said.

For some reason the simple conversation pained Cecily. What had been between them? What had caused them to break up?

Behind her Marcus surveyed the food and leaned forward to whisper near her ear. "What did you bring today, Miss Blake, besides a sissified city boy, I mean?"

She decided to ignore the last part and answer the first. "I brought that, and that, and that, and that." She pointed to all the food she had prepared.

"Your cook really outdid herself this year, dear, the food is excellent," Mrs. Henshaw interrupted.

Cecily started to tell her she had made the food herself, but that would mean admitting they could no longer afford to keep their cook. "Thank you," she said instead.

"But," Radley started, but Cecily squeezed his bicep to keep him from speaking. He pressed his lips together and kept silent. He was becoming used to the fact that the country life had different rules than the ones he normally lived by.

"Not much there to squeeze," Marcus whispered.

"You're being rude," she whispered.

"Me?" he asked innocently and pointed to himself.

She decided the best course of action was to ignore him, so she turned her back on him and ushered Radley to a table. She probably could have predicted Marcus would sit across from them, and that also meant she would be subjected to his perfect girlfriend.

"I'm afraid I don't remember your name," Lacey said to Cecily.

"This is Lee," Marcus answered for her. "And her friend Bradley."

"Radley," Radley corrected him.

"Lee," Lacey said. Her nose wrinkled delicately in distaste. "That's an interesting name."

"I didn't know anyone called you that," Radley said.

"They don't," Cecily said. "My name is Cecily," she said to Lacey.

"Are you from one of the Native American tribes around here?" Lacey asked. Beside her Marcus choked on a sip of iced tea.

"No, my maternal grandparents are from Spain."

"I didn't realize your lineage was that closely associated with Spain," Marcus said with some fascination. "Do you speak Spanish?"

"Only what I learned in school," Cecily said. "My mother is fluent, although she doesn't speak it much and she doesn't have an accent. Unless she's angry, and then she says a stream of words I'm probably not allowed to repeat. She used to say them a lot when she lived here." She smiled at Marcus and he returned it.

"Your mom is the best. You remind me of her," Radley said.

Cecily took a bite and swallowed before answering. She and her mother didn't exactly hate each other, but they butted heads frequently. "People usually say I'm more like my dad."

"Maybe," Radley conceded. "I guess I didn't know him as well."

"How do you know her mother and not her father?" Lacey asked.

"I live in Chicago where her mother lives," Radley answered.

"Oh." Lacey looked around. "Is your father here?"

Cecily wondered if it was a calculated question. Surely someone would have filled her in on the gossip about her father.

"No," Cecily said. She concentrated on her food.

"Where is he?" Lacey persisted.

"Victorville, California," Cecily replied. It was the nearest medium security federal prison.

"What's he doing there?" Lacey asked.

"Lacey, could you possibly be any more nosey?" Marcus said it teasingly, but Cecily caught the hint of warning in his tone, and so did Lacey, apparently, because she didn't ask any more. Instead she turned her attention to Radley.

"What do you do, Radley?"

Marcus looked at him in interest, too.

"I wrote a computer program that's a new metasearch system," he said.

"That sounds lucrative," Lacey said.

"Not yet, but I have high hopes." He finished his food and rested his arm on the back of Cecily's chair.

"How long are you staying?" Marcus blurted.

"I guess that's up to Cecily," Radley said. He picked up a strand of her hair and twined it around his finger. "I would stay forever if she'd let me."

Cecily looked at him and realized he meant it. Across from them Marcus jabbed his fork into his plate so hard it snapped in half.

CHAPTER 7

"*L*et's go for a walk," Cecily suggested. She felt a confrontation looming and she needed to get Radley away before it happened.

"All right," Radley said. He stood to clear his trash and took her plate, too.

"Have fun, you kids," Lacey called.

Thanks, grandma, Cecily wanted to say. Of course Lacey was only twenty six, but that was still six years older than her. She had to admit the girl wasn't hideous. At least not during their most recent encounter, but she still refused to like her. If she liked her, she would feel guilty for all the time she had spent with Marcus.

"My opinion of your neighbor hasn't changed," Radley said. "I still think he's odd. And hostile."

Cecily kept silent. The last thing she wanted right now was to talk about Marcus.

"Where are we going?" Radley asked.

Cecily stopped and looked around. She had been walking without purpose or direction. "I don't know. Is there anywhere you want to see?"

"Somewhere private," he said. "I feel like we haven't had a moment alone together since I arrived."

"Privacy shouldn't be hard to find on a ranch this size," Cecily said. She turned and started to walk again.

"This is a massive ranch. I thought your ranch was huge until I came here. I've never seen so much land or so many cows." He took her hand. "How is the horse business progressing?"

"Good," Cecily said. She launched into a long explanation of her new business until she realized his eyes were glazed over. "I'm sorry, Radley, I'm boring you."

"You're not boring me," Radley said. "I'm not up on my horse jargon. Sorry."

"I'm sure it would be the same if you tried to describe to me what you do for a living."

"No, then you really would be bored. I'm bored by it, and it's my life."

They laughed together.

He pulled her to a stop and positioned her against a fencepost. "This looks sufficiently deserted." He settled his hands on her waist and her heart started to thud in anticipation. If this kiss was half as good as the one she shared with Marcus, then they would have a happy future together, indeed.

"I've waited a long time for this," Radley whispered. "Too long." He cupped her face with his hands. His mouth slowly descended toward hers.

"Hey, this is a surprise."

Cecily's eyes flew open. Radley looked as surprised and irritated as she felt. "Marcus," she muttered. She turned her head to look at him. She had no doubt he had followed them to preempt their kiss.

He sat atop his stallion, blatant amusement written on his face. "I'm sorry, did I interrupt something?"

"What are you doing here?" Cecily asked.

"Here? On my property? Where I have every right to be? I thought it was a nice day for a ride."

"Where's Lacey, your super serious longtime girlfriend?"

"Around here somewhere. Can I give you a lift back to the house?" He held out a hand to her.

"No thank you," she said between her teeth. How was she ever going to explain his behavior to Radley? She tugged his arm. "Let's keep walking."

"Sounds good," Marcus said.

"I wasn't talking to you," she threw over her shoulder.

"I feel duty bound to protect you both while you're on my land. Your boyfriend isn't used to the dangers of Montana wilderness."

"At this point I'm fairly certain I could take down a grizzly with my bare hands," she called.

"All the same, I'd feel much better if I accompanied you. I wouldn't want you to land yourself in a situation you're unprepared for," Marcus said.

"Is there something going on here I should know about?" Radley asked.

"Tell him, Lee," Marcus urged.

"No," Cecily said. "There's nothing to tell."

"Sure there is," Marcus said. "We've had some trouble in these parts with criminals. It's not safe to go walking alone in the woods."

She hesitated because she heard the sincerity in his tone. She had forgotten Mathew's killer was still on the loose and might be roaming the woods around the house.

"That's true," she said. She hesitated and looked at Radley. "Maybe we should go back," she said apologetically.

"If you think so," he said. He smiled and took her hand again.

"Young love," Marcus said in a false, dreamy tone. "So innocent." He turned his horse so he was now walking in front of them.

"*Weird*," Radley mouthed.

Cecily's answering smile was halfhearted. Radley didn't understand Marcus's hidden meaning, but she did. *Innocent and lacking passion*, was what he meant, as clearly as if he had said it. The most galling part of it was that she wasn't sure she disagreed. She had almost found out how high the level of chemistry between her and Radley was when Marcus interrupted them. She clenched her fists and glared at a spot off to her right. He didn't want her, not really, but he didn't want anyone else to have her, either. He was maddening.

When they reached the house, Kitty and Dante were standing outside the barn talking.

"Radley, I'm not sure I'm going to invite you back if you disappear into the wilderness with my little sister," Dante teased. Of course Cecily knew he was joking. He and Radley were close. There was nothing Dante would like better than for him and Cecily to get together.

"Don't worry," Marcus said as he easily slid off his horse. "I protected her virtue for you." He tossed his reins to a stable hand and breezed into the barn.

"What was that about?" Dante asked.

"Don't ask," Cecily said.

"That guy is creepy," Radley said. "I think he's stalking Cecily."

Dante and Kitty laughed weakly and looked at Cecily in question.

"Who can understand the Henshaws?" she asked, and then cast about for a distraction. "Let's play horseshoes."

They played until it was time for the fireworks. She spread out a blanket she had brought from home and sat close by Radley. For a while they watched the fireworks in silence, and then he turned to her and took her hand.

"Cecily, I want to talk to you about something. I've been trying to find the right time and the right words all week, but it hasn't happened. Maybe the darkness and the fireworks will give me the cover I need." He took a deep breath. "I've had an offer on my product from one of the big guns in the industry. I'm about to make a killing and become very wealthy."

"Radley, that's great. Congratulations."

He smiled. "Thanks, although that wasn't what I wanted to tell you. The point is that I'm about to retire. I'm available to relocate, and I want to come here. We've danced around the issue of us for three years now, but you have to know how I feel about you. I think it's time we give us a chance." A firework exploded and lit up the sky. He settled his hand on her waist and leaned in to kiss her. When the kiss ended she opened her eyes and looked over his shoulder.

Marcus was staring at her, and by the look on his face she knew he had heard every word.

CHAPTER 8

*C*ecily decided to spend a rare day cocooned inside her house, wrapped in self pity. Dante and Kitty had just left to take Radley back to the airport. At the last minute they decided to fly back to Chicago with him and spend a few days with Dante and Cecily's mother, Shelby.

It was two days since July fourth and she had tried, really tried to involve herself with Radley. For the last two days they kissed and cuddled like any normal couple. Cecily thought maybe if she gave it some time they would develop the passion she shared with Marcus, but in the end she couldn't keep up the charade any longer. The night before, Radley had finally addressed the situation between them.

"You can't be with me, can you?" Radley asked.

Cecily shook her head. Her eyes were full of tears that clouded her vision. "I'm sorry. I never wanted to hurt you."

"I'm disappointed, not hurt. There's a difference. We're still friends."

"You're one in a million, Radley," she said.

"But not the one for you."

She shook her head again.

"Don't tell me; it's the deranged cowboy."

She sniffled and wiped her eyes. "I'm afraid so."

"Well, at least that explains his semi-psychotic, antisocial behavior." He kissed her cheek. "Good luck, Cecily."

She hugged him tightly. "Thanks, Radley. I truly am sorry things didn't work out. A part of me always wondered if you were the one. I hope you find a great girl."

After that he and Dante had stayed up half the night talking. She didn't think it was her imagination when she read accusation in Dante's eyes before he left for the airport. He wasn't happy things hadn't worked out between Cecily and Radley, especially after the two couples had spent time together all week and had fun.

For a moment, Cecily wondered how Marcus would fit into the family dynamic with Dante and Kitty, but then shook her head to clear it. It didn't matter. Marcus was with Lacey, presumably for life. Eventually she would either get over him or learn to live without him.

A knock sounded at her door. She knew by the strength of it that it was a man. *What now*, she wondered, sure it was one of the hands with a question. But it wasn't. It was Marcus.

She opened the door and for a long moment they looked at each other.

"Is he gone?" he asked at last.

"Yes," she said.

"For good?"

She hated to admit the truth, but she couldn't lie. "Yes."

He continued to stare at her in silence a few beats before sweeping aside the door, pulling her into his arms, and kissing her with all the intensity that had been building between them the last few weeks. She stood on her toes to get closer to him and twined her fingers in his hair. His palms were flat against her back, pressing her closer. When they couldn't get any closer, he lifted her, pinning her in place so they were eye level. He deepened the kiss and she trembled with the intensity of it.

He started to walk, but she was too far gone to notice until he spoke.

"Which way?"

"Which way what?" she murmured against his lips.

"To your bedroom."

Her eyes popped open, but he wasn't looking at her. He had stopped walking to kiss her again and his eyes were closed.

"Stop," she said. She had to say it again before it registered. She shoved away from him and jumped out of his embrace.

"Lee, what's wrong?"

"This," she said furiously.

"What?" He sounded truly confused.

"*This*," she said more insistently. She pointed between them. "You and me. I told you I'm not going to be what you want, Marcus."

He crossed his arms over his chest. "And what is that?"

Her face blushed crimson, but she had to get the words out. "Your mistress."

His scowl was impressively scary. "Who said anything about that?"

"You did, by your actions. Coming here in the middle of the day and trying to carry me to my bedroom." Now she crossed her arms over her chest.

"Since when does that make me a bad person? It's doing what comes naturally."

"Maybe for some people," she said.

Her rejection stung and made him lash out at her. "Don't tell me you're saving yourself for marriage," he smirked.

She raised her chin. "So what if I am?"

He started to laugh before realizing she was serious. "Lee, you mean it? You've never…" He let the words trail off and she was glad he didn't finish the sentence. No need to spell out the obvious and further her discomfort.

"No, I've never. I've kissed a large portion of the male population, but that's as far as I've ever gone. Some of us have morals, you know."

His wondrous expression was replaced by a frown. "What's that supposed to mean?"

"I think it's obvious." She pivoted around him and strode to the door. "You might as well go. It's clear you're not going to get what you're after because I'm not doing that," she pointed to the bedroom, "until I'm married."

Except for the fact that he turned to look at her he made no move to leave. For a long, silent moment he stared at her. "Then marry me," he said softly.

She blew out a breath. "Marcus, please don't tease me about this. I'm not going to budge on this point. I'm very serious."

"So am I."

"No you're not," she argued.

"Yes I am," he said.

"Don't be ridiculous," she said. Her voice faltered and her eyes filled with tears. She couldn't believe he was toying with her this way.

He went forward and gathered her hands in his. "Lee, I'm not kidding. I want you to marry me. Now. Today."

She searched his face. She didn't see any traces of humor. "You're serious," she whispered.

He nodded and dropped to his knees in front of her. "Cecily Blake, will you marry me?"

She blinked at him in confusion. "Why?"

"Because I honestly don't think I can live without you, and I don't want to find out. Please." He kissed her hands.

"All right." She couldn't believe it when she heard herself agree, and then she couldn't believe how right it felt. Shouldn't she be panicking right now? She didn't feel panic, though, she felt elation.

He must have felt some elation, too, because he stood and kissed her with such enthusiasm it knocked her back against the wall. He pressed a palm to the wall on either side of her and let go of everything he had been holding back until she had to grasp his shirt to keep herself standing.

"You're killing me," she told him.

He smiled that cocky smile men get when they know they've knocked a woman's socks off. "This is only the beginning. Let's go." He took her hand and started to lead her from the house.

"I need to pack." She tried to tug her hand out of his grasp.

He shook his head and kept walking. "I'm not giving you the opportunity to change your mind. We'll buy what you need there."

"Where is there?" She had to sprint to keep up with him.

"Las Vegas, of course," he said matter-of-factly.

"Of course," she repeated, rolling her eyes at his back.

"I saw that," he said.

They reached his truck. He kissed her, picked her up, and tossed her in the cab. She started to laugh at the insanity of it all and then couldn't stop. This day was rapidly turning out to be the strangest and best day of her life.

arcus's hurry when they were in Montana turned into patience when they reached Las Vegas. Cecily had assumed they would find the first available wedding chapel and head to a hotel, but she was wrong.

"Here is my credit card," he said as he handed her a tiny rectangle marked "Platinum." "I want you to buy a dress and whatever else you need. Get your hair and makeup done and anything else you want." He turned to go.

"Where are you going?" she asked in a sudden panic. Was he having second thoughts?

He turned back to her with a smile. "I'm going to plan our wedding." He pressed his palm to her cheek, and then he was gone.

She stared after him with a loopy grin on her face.

"That's a fine looking hunk of man meat." The woman who had spoken looked official, as if she worked for the store, so Cecily was surprised by her words. She didn't disagree, though.

"Yes he is."

"How long have you two been together?"

Cecily checked her watch. "About four hours."

"One of *those* couples. Don't worry; we get that a lot. I suppose you'll need the works."

"I have no idea what the works are, but since I came here with the clothes I'm wearing, I think you're probably right."

The woman laughed and took her hand. "Right this way. What's your name?"

"Lee," Cecily answered impulsively.

"Lee," the woman repeated. "I'm Angela, and I'll be at your beck and call today, more because I saw your fiancé flash a platinum card than because I actually like you." She winked at Cecily to let her know she was kidding.

By the end of the day, Cecily thought Angela was amazing. She somehow found a wedding dress that perfectly suited Cecily's coloring and style and then had it tailored so it looked like it was made for her. She set her up with a stylist who did her hair and makeup, then outfitted her with lingerie and clothes for the next three days. She also loaded a cosmetic bag with all the toiletries and makeup Cecily would need. It had been so long since she went shopping that she wanted to weep with the joy of it all. Instead she hugged Angela tightly and kissed her cheek.

"Can I keep you?" she asked.

"Only if we can share your hunky man," Angela said.

Cecily let her go. "See you later, stranger."

When Marcus arrived she was waiting in the lobby, wearing her beautiful dress and holding her two new suitcases.

He whistled appreciatively and she stared with the same appreciation. He was wearing a tuxedo and carrying a beautiful bouquet of flowers, which he presented to her before he kissed her.

"Ready?" he asked. The question was loaded, and she knew he was giving her the opportunity to change her mind.

"I'm ready," she said, laying her hand on his arm to stop him. "Are you ready? Are you sure you don't want to wait until your family can join us? I hate to take your marriage away from them. They should be here, I think."

He rested his hand on hers. "They've gone through so much lately. I don't think they're up to the public spectacle of a wedding, and I don't want to wait until they are. I want to be with you. Today."

Her heart fluttered at his bluntness. She had a moment's hesitation, not because she doubted her feelings, but because she doubted his. Was this simply lust on his part, or a desire to acquire what he couldn't have? After the ceremony would he find an excuse to have it annulled and toss her away like yesterday's garbage? She wasn't sure she knew him well enough to answer that question. But she did know she wanted to be with him as much as or more than he wanted to be with her. It was a start, and for now she hoped it would be enough.

She took a step toward the door, but this time he was the one to halt her. "What about your family? Do you want them to be here?"

She thought about that. She wanted her father to walk her down the aisle, as she had always dreamed, but he had eight years left on his prison sentence. There was no way she was going to wait that long. Dante would make a nice substitute, but a public wedding might stir up the controversy surrounding her family. Especially if she married a Henshaw. She wouldn't do that to them.

"No," she said with certainty. "I want it like this."

He nodded, took her hand, and twined their fingers together. Out of nowhere she had the thought that this was the first time they had ever held hands in such a manner, and in a few short minutes he would be her husband.

Am I crazy? she asked herself. The answer was an unequivocal *yes*, but she still couldn't stop. She wanted to marry Marcus right now, and if there were repercussions, she would deal with them as they arose.

He led her to a chapel decorated tastefully with flowers to match her bouquet. He had also rented a limousine and hired a photographer.

She bit her lip as she looked around the flower-strewn chapel, and he noticed.

"What?" he asked.

"I feel bad you're footing the bill for our wedding."

He smiled. "Do you know how easily I'm getting off? If we had a traditional wedding, I would have to foot the bill for a rehearsal dinner that would probably cost more than this wedding."

"Still," she said, nervously nibbling her thumb.

He took her hand and held it. "Stop worrying and stop being so proud. You're almost my wife. What's mine is yours now."

"Something tells me if the shoe was on the other foot and I was the one paying all the bills you wouldn't be happy."

"That's because I'm a man. I'm supposed to provide for you."

Their names were called before she could protest. Certainly he didn't expect her to observe the traditional role of a woman and stay at home to raise babies. Maybe someday she would be content in that capacity, but right now she had a ranch and a business to run.

She walked down the aisle and tried not to be sad that she wasn't on her father's arm. The photographer took dozens of pictures of her progress.

At the front of the chapel Marcus stood smiling brilliantly. Right now he looked like he had forever on his mind, and Cecily stored the vision away for later inspection.

"Do you, Marcus Dylan Henshaw take this Cecily Alandra Jacinta Diaz Blake to be your lawfully wedded wife?" the preacher said.

Marcus smiled. "So long as I never have to memorize her name, then yes."

The preacher stifled a laugh, cleared his throat, and continued. "And do you Cecily Alandra Jacinta Diaz Blake take this Marcus Dylan Henshaw to be your lawfully wedded husband?"

There was a pregnant pause while Cecily searched her heart and mind once more. "I do," she said. Marcus sagged slightly in relief.

"Repeat after me," the minister said, and then stated their vows. They each repeated his words and Marcus slipped a ring on her finger. She was momentarily stunned by the largess of the diamond and platinum band. For a second she felt bad he had purchased his own wedding ring, but when she slipped it on his finger and felt the light caress of his hand against hers, she forgot everything else.

"By the power vested in me by the city of Las Vegas and the state of Nevada, I now declare you man and wife. Marcus, you may kiss your bride."

"Cecily Alandra Jacinta Diaz Blake *Henshaw*," Marcus muttered, and then he kissed her.

CHAPTER 10

*C*ecily's wedding elation lasted exactly thirty seconds before turning to abject terror.

"Do you want to grab a bite to eat?" Marcus asked.

She sagged in relief because one more thing now stood between her and her wedding night. All she could think was, *I'm not ready for this, and he's practically a stranger.* She felt like she might be sick. If he noticed her hand in his was trembling, he was too polite to comment. He did run a soothing hand down her back, so he must have sensed some of her fear.

"Relax," he whispered. He put his arm around her and pulled her to rest against him. They rode in comfortable silence and she was disappointed when they reached the restaurant. She thought she could stay in Marcus's arms forever. Reluctantly, she ripped herself away and allowed the limo driver to help her from the car.

"You sure know how to treat a lady, Marcus," Cecily said when they were seated inside the seedy looking hot dog joint.

He looked around at the place with fresh eyes. "I'm sorry. I came here last time I was in town and enjoyed it. We'll go someplace nicer." He would have stood but she grabbed his hand and tugged him back down.

"I was teasing you. This looks more like my kind of place. I'm a fan of hot dogs and out of the way restaurants."

"Me too," he said. They shared a smile, glad to have one thing in common.

The silence at supper was awkward, but Cecily chalked it up to nerves, at least on her part.

"This is sort of our first date," Marcus said when he couldn't take the silence any more. He smiled.

"You have a dimple." She touched her finger to his cheek. His hair was sandy blond, and his eyes were dark blue. He looked like a Ken doll.

"You have two." He touched both his index fingers to her cheeks. "And twelve names."

She chuckled. "The Spanish part of me had to come out somewhere. We Spanish like our names."

"My wife is exotic." He arched an eyebrow at her.

"I'm your wife," she exclaimed.

"Yes, you are. Are you sad about that?"

"No," she said. She picked up his hand and squeezed it. "Surprised. Yesterday we weren't even dating."

He leaned forward and kissed her lightly on the lips. "I've never done anything this impulsive before."

"I've done lots of impulsive things, but I've been trying to outgrow my old ways."

"I like you," he said.

"I should hope so. You married me," she said.

"No, I mean I really like you." He brushed her hair off her face. "You're fun and spunky, passionate and interesting. You can't imagine my surprise that day we kissed. It was like my blinders were removed, and I really saw you for the first time. All these years, you've been right under my nose, and I didn't even know."

She smiled, charmed by his sweet words. "Those things you listed are first impressions. I hope you still like me when you get to know me better."

"We've known each other for twenty years," Marcus said. "How many skeletons do you think we have hiding in our closets?"

"You know me, but you don't *know* me," she leaned close and lowered her voice.

He leaned forward so they sat elbow to elbow across from each other. "I've heard that somewhere before."

She closed the gap between them and kissed him, not caring who saw.

"Ready to go?" he asked.

She froze, all of her bravado fleeing. "I'm not sure I'll ever be ready."

He smiled. "Come on, we'll take it slowly. You'll be fine."

She nodded and stood, trying hard to calm the frantic beating of her heart. Was every woman this afraid on her wedding night, or was it because Marcus was a relative stranger? She had kissed him fewer times than she could count on two hands, and now she was going to be as intimate with him as two people could be.

The short drive to their hotel was once again awkward, but this time neither of them tried to relieve the awkwardness.

Marcus paid a bellhop to carry their bags to their room and then they were alone with the large bed looming in front of them.

"I think I'm supposed to change my clothes now," Cecily said, hating the way her voice quavered nervously.

"It's our honeymoon, you can do whatever you want," Marcus said. His tone was reassuring and she took a deep breath.

"I want to change," she said.

"All right. I'll change, too."

She nodded and dragged her suitcase into the bathroom with her. If her hair and makeup weren't perfect from her time at the salon, she would shower, but she didn't want to mess up what the stylists had worked so hard to create. Instead she freshened up in the sink, brushed her teeth twice, touched up her makeup, and changed into the beautiful lingerie Angela had picked out for her. It was a creamy white concoction that barely covered her and yet still managed to look classy.

I can do this, she told herself. Countless generations of women had done this before her. It was no big deal. *If it's no big deal, why do you feel like you're going to throw up,* she wondered, and then pushed the thought away. She took a deep breath, squeezed her eyes shut, then opened them and stepped through the door.

Marcus was lying on the bed. He had stripped down to his boxer shorts and he was watching a game on television. Whatever the game was it wasn't enough to hold his interest, because as soon as he heard the door, he snapped off the television and looked at Cecily.

He sat up and opened his arms to her and she stumbled forward.

"You look like something from a dream," he told her. He put his arms around her and dragged her across him so she was lying on the bed beside him. "I've always thought you were a beautiful girl, but today I know for certain you are the loveliest woman I have ever seen." He reverently caressed her cheek with the tips of his fingers.

"You've always thought I was beautiful?" she asked in a small, scared voice.

He nodded. "I watched you grow up, remember. I was surprised Mathew didn't go for you. Maggie's pretty, but she has nothing on you."

She smiled at him.

"I'm not sure why the possibility of having you for myself didn't occur to me until recently."

"Maybe because until recently it would have been illegal," she suggested, and giggled when he pinched her waist. He leaned in to kiss her and she stopped giggling.

"Relax," he said gently when she trembled beneath him.

"I'm sorry," she said. "I'm a little nervous."

"I'm nervous too," he admitted.

That surprised her. "Haven't you done this before?"

"Yes, but I've never been anyone's first. I want things to go well for you, and it's sort of awe-inspiring you're my wife and that you waited for me."

She hadn't thought of it in those terms. She *had* waited for her husband in order to make a gift of her body, but she hadn't recognized the fact that this man beside her was now her husband. *He* would be the one claiming the gift she was presenting. Clarifying the facts in her mind worked to push away her nerves. She smiled shyly at him as he bent to kiss her again, and this time when she trembled it wasn't from fear.

CHAPTER 11

"Perfect" was the word Cecily would use to describe the three days she and Marcus spent in Las Vegas. It was a honeymoon in every sense of the word, more so because no one knew where they were or what they were doing. They felt like they had captured their own piece of paradise as they hid away from the world and explored their new relationship.

For three days they spent almost every moment together. Neither of them wanted to return home, but both of them had responsibilities to tend to. And they had to face their families and friends.

"Where did you tell your parents you went?" she asked. So far, they had talked about everything except what would happen when they returned home.

"Away. I'm twenty six; I don't answer to them about every detail of my life. Where does your family think you are?"

"No one is home. Dante and Kitty are in Chicago with my mom. I called my foreman to let him know I would be gone for a few days and told him what to do in my absence."

"He didn't know already?" he asked.

She didn't like his teasing tone. "I'm sure he did, but I'm the one he reports to, and I give the orders."

He leaned in to kiss her cheek. "You're cute when you get on your high horse."

She dropped her suitcase when he pulled her further into his embrace. "We're going to miss our airplane."

"Doesn't matter, no one is expecting us anyway." He backed her up to the bed and then they heard the housekeeper opening the door. He groaned. "And so it begins with the interruptions." He stepped back and picked up her suitcase. "Come on, Lee, let's go home."

The problem, she realized when they arrived back in their small town, was that they hadn't agreed where home was.

"Do you want to stop by your place and check on things before we head home?" he asked.

"I thought my place was home," she said.

"Your spread is an hour's drive from our ranch. I can't commute that far every day."

"But you expect me to?" she asked. She was working hard to rein in her temper. It was a misunderstanding, that was all. "Besides, once Dante goes back to work in Omaha we'll be alone at my house. *Alone*," she stretched out the word. "Me and you. Together. By ourselves."

He clasped her hand. "That sounds wonderful, but I can't leave my parents so soon after they lost Mathew. Mom especially isn't doing well." He glanced at her out of the corner of his eye. "Do you have to go to your place every day? Can you get away with going a few times a week?"

She looked out the window. She didn't want to. Her business was new, and she needed to be there every day. On the other hand, her foreman was capable and trustworthy, and she didn't want to hurt Marcus's parents by taking him away from them.

"I suppose," she mumbled.

He picked up her hand and kissed it. "Thanks. In a few years when we're ready for kids, we'll work something out so that we'll have a place of our own."

All the blood drained from her face and she froze in horror. In her haste and nervousness she hadn't considered birth control. "Uh, Marcus," she said.

He turned to her in concern. "What is it, Lee? Are you all right, honey?"

She couldn't tell him. He might be angry with her for not taking care of it. Obviously he had assumed she was prepared because he didn't mention protection, either. He was more experienced in these matters, so probably the women he had been with actually were prepared.

"Nothing." She smiled and hoped it looked convincing. It was probably all right anyway. Her doctor had warned her that because of her irregular menstrual cycle getting pregnant might be a challenge for her. She would go to the doctor as soon as possible and ask to be put on some form of birth control.

They arrived at her house. She spoke with her foreman, checked on her horses, and spent some time packing up essentials to take to the Henshaw's. As she was finishing, she heard a car in the drive and knew by the rumble of the engine that it was Kitty and Dante.

"You guys are home early," she said as she went out on the porch to greet them.

"Mom had to go away on business, and we didn't want to stay in Chicago alone. So we decided to come home," Dante said. He eyed Marcus's truck. "Is a Henshaw here? Are they buying something else?"

"Uh," Cecily said. She had no idea how to tell her brother and best friend she was now a Henshaw.

"Lee, let's make sure and take these with us," Marcus said. He exited the bedroom dangling her laciest pair of black underwear from one finger, and froze with them held in midair as he stared at Dante and Kitty and they stared at him.

"What exactly is he buying?" Kitty asked in her wry way that usually made Dante and Cecily laugh. Now it only added to the tension.

"Um," Cecily started again. She snatched her underpants out of Marcus's hand and stuffed it in her pocket. "Don't you dare laugh," she told him because she could see the corners of his mouth turning up. She turned back to Kitty and Dante. "Come inside, we have something to discuss."

They trooped up the stairs behind her and sat nervously on the couch. She sat across from them on the love seat. Marcus sat next to her. Kitty and Dante looked curiously between them.

"I'm going to cut to the chase here and ask why you were holding a pair of my sister's underpants," Dante said. "A pair I could have lived without knowing she owned."

"Long story short, we're married," Cecily blurted.

Marcus started to chuckle. "I think maybe they're going to need the long version."

"The longest version possible," Kitty said, and Marcus laughed again.

"I'm not sure where to begin," Cecily said. She looked at Marcus for help.

"I'm not either," he said. "It's a complicated story neither of us understands. Suffice it to say we're married and have every intention of staying that way." He clasped Cecily's hand and held onto it tightly, a determined expression on his face.

Kitty and Dante remained speechless. Their pupils were fixed and dilated from the shock.

"Are you pregnant?" Dante asked at last.

Cecily's mouth fell and her cheeks flushed. "Dante! No, I never, we didn't, I mean…Kitty," she said pleadingly, and looked at her best friend for help.

Kitty leaned over to whisper something in Dante's ear, most likely the fact that Cecily was a virgin and remained that way until her wedding night because he relaxed visibly.

"That's a relief," he said out loud. "And a bit of a surprise, really."

"Dante," Cecily said again. Beside her Marcus chuckled again. She scowled at him.

"What? It was a relief and a surprise to me, too," he said.

Kitty laughed, and the sound went a long way toward clearing some of the tension from the atmosphere. "Let's have some iced tea and continue this conversation. I'll help you pour, Cecily." She stood, grabbed Cecily's hand, and dragged her into the kitchen. Behind them Dante and Marcus made awkward small talk.

"Okay, what is going on?" Kitty whispered when they reached the kitchen.

Cecily drew in a breath and let it out slowly. "I honestly don't know how to explain," Cecily said.

"Try, Cecily, for the sake of my sanity, you have to try," Kitty said earnestly.

"We found that we share a sort of connection. A chemistry, really. We were attracted to each other, so much that we couldn't stay apart. So he asked me to marry him when he found out I don't you-know-what outside of marriage."

Kitty's eyes were troubled, and no wonder. Cecily wasn't doing a good job of conveying the story.

"Do you love him?" Kitty asked.

"I," Cecily paused. "I do," she said softly. "With all my heart. I'm totally in love with him," she said it in a shocked tone and then sat down at the table because her legs would no longer support her.

"You didn't know before you married him?"

Cecily shook her head. "There wasn't time to think about it, and maybe I wasn't. But the last three days cemented whatever I felt for him. I love him," she repeated again. She looked up at Kitty and smiled. "I totally love my husband."

Kitty leaned down, hugged her around the neck, and kissed her forehead. "Be happy, Cecily. And if you're not, if you ever need me, I'm always here for you; I'll do anything to help you."

Cecily hugged her waist. "Thanks, Kitty. Sorry I got married before you."

"With two older sisters who are already married I sort of gave up trying to be first at things."

They poured iced tea and took it to the men who hadn't progressed past their awkward small talk.

"What's your full name, Dante?" Marcus asked as he sipped his iced tea.

"Dante Adan Javier Diaz Blake," Dante said.

Marcus clasped Cecily's hand. "We're not doing that to our kids."

"We'll talk," she replied, and then felt a small flutter of worry when she realized she might be carrying one of their children right now.

CHAPTER 12

If Cecily was nervous about telling her brother about her hasty nuptials, it was nothing compared to the abject terror she felt at telling Marcus's parents.

Marcus pulled off the road before they reached his house and took Cecily in his arms. "It's going to be all right. My parents will be shocked, but they'll get over it, and they'll love you. It's not like you're a stranger to them; our families have been neighbors for generations."

She snuggled into his embrace. "Can't we stay right here? We'll live in your truck."

"Don't be a coward," he said. "Where's my little fireball?"

"She's never had to face in-laws before. You're so lucky my dad's in prison."

"Your mom's not."

"My mom will take one look at you and ask why I didn't marry you sooner."

"I've been asking myself that same question. Why *didn't* you marry me sooner?"

"Because you didn't ask," she said. He kissed her and it was awhile before they got on the road again.

When they pulled in front of his house, though, they faced another hurdle.

"Uh-oh," Marcus said.

Lacey opened the front door and stepped onto the porch.

"I guess I'd better break up with my girlfriend," he said sheepishly.

"You think so?" Cecily asked peevishly. She crossed her arms over her chest.

"I'll make this up to you later."

"Don't promise her the same thing," she said, only half joking.

He rolled his eyes at her and exited the truck.

She remained in the safety of the truck and watched the drama unfold. Lacey bounded off the porch and attempted to throw her arms around him, but Marcus held up a hand to halt her. She stopped and made a pouty face at him. He said something and motioned behind him to his truck. Cecily crouched down so she could barely see out. Lacey looked at the truck in bewilderment. She shook her head and screamed something at Marcus. He replied in a calm tone. She screamed again and pointed to the ring finger of her left hand. He said something else and shook his head. She slapped him hard across the face. Although Cecily hated to see him hurt in any way, a part of her had to admit he had it coming.

Lacey slammed into her car and sped off down the long lane. Before she was out of sight she rolled down her window and made a rude gesture with her hand.

Marcus strolled over to Cecily and opened the passenger door of the truck.

"She hit me," he said.

"Yes, I saw," Cecily said. She drew him close and kissed the area where a hand-shaped welt now stood. "Quite a lady you had there."

He laughed, then winced and touched his cheek. "Quite a lady I have here," he said tenderly. He drew her forward and kissed her, not caring that a dozen ranch hands were buzzing around watching everything.

She kissed him in return, totally forgetting time and place, at least until his parents chose that moment to make an appearance.

His father cleared his throat.

"Marcus?" his mother said questioningly.

Marcus pulled back to smile at Cecily who was blushing crimson. "Mom, Dad," he said. "Let's go inside." He lifted Cecily out of the truck and didn't let her go. "Have to make it official," he whispered. He carried her over the threshold and set her down, all while his parents were trailing behind them looking shell-shocked.

They sat down in the same formation they had sat earlier with Kitty and Dante, and Mr. and Mrs. Henshaw wore similar expressions of shock and alarm.

"You may have noticed Lacey and I broke up," Marcus said. Mr. and Mrs. Henshaw nodded. "What you aren't aware of is the fact that Cecily and I are now married."

Mr. Henshaw's eyes bugged. Mrs. Henshaw gasped.

"Marcus, you can't be serious," she said.

"I am serious, Mother. I know it seems sudden to you, but this has been brewing between us for a couple of years. Recent events have made me realize I don't want to go on without her, that I can't go on without her." He squeezed Cecily's hand. She returned his grip until it was painful.

"Is there a baby?" Mrs. Henshaw asked, avoiding Cecily's gaze and focusing instead on her son.

Marcus expelled a frustrated breath. "No," he said, shaking his head vehemently. "Cecily's not that type of girl."

"But this is sudden, and there was no wedding. What are we going to tell people?"

"The truth," Marcus said. "We ran off to Las Vegas and got married."

"But people will think what I did. They'll think you had to get married," Mrs. Henshaw said.

"And when no baby appears in nine months they'll know that wasn't the reason," he said.

Cecily's stomach turned over. What if there *was* a baby in nine months? What if she had gotten pregnant on her honeymoon? No one would ever believe they hadn't jumped the gun, least of all Marcus's mother.

"I know this is a shock to you both," Marcus said gently. "But we wanted to get married as soon as possible, and I didn't want to put you through the fiasco of a wedding so soon after everything that has happened. I realize it's going to be an adjustment, but you're going to have to come to terms with the fact that Cecily is my wife. Forever."

Mr. and Mrs. Henshaw still sat unblinking and silent. Finally Mr. Henshaw slapped his hand on his knee.

"Well, it's about time someone married one of the neighbors. Welcome to the family, little Cecily Blake. Boy, let's go unload her stuff." He stood and Marcus followed him out of the room.

Cecily watched them go with a smile. That had gone better than she could have hoped. If the speed of their whirlwind courtship was the only problem, the longevity would eventually win them over. No one had mentioned the age difference, or the fact that Cecily's father was in prison, or her penniless state. When she turned back to Mrs. Henshaw, though, her smile fled. The older woman was looking at her with something like malice.

"I don't know what you did to trap my son into this marriage, but I can promise you I'm going to do everything in my power to get him out of it."

CHAPTER 13

When Marcus showed her to their room that night, Cecily intended to have a serious talk with him, but then he turned on the radio and kissed her and she forgot everything else.

"What's the radio for?" she murmured against his lips.

"Noise control," he said, causing her to laugh until he kissed her again.

Awhile later he gave her the tour of his bedroom. She was glad to see it was more like a suite with a large sleeping room, sitting area, and full bathroom with double sinks.

"I was picturing a teenager's room with band posters and pictures of supermodels," she said.

"That's what Mathew's room looks like," he said, swallowing hard.

"I'm sorry you're hurting, Marcus," she said gently.

"You make it better," he said. He put an arm around her and pulled her close. "I think it went well with Mom and Dad."

Her brow wrinkled. She wasn't sure how to tell him he couldn't be farther from the truth. She had learned from her brother men were sensitive about their mothers. In Dante's eyes their mother could do no wrong.

"It seems like your dad has accepted me," she said.

Marcus ran his fingers lightly up and down her arm. "Mmm, hmm."

"Did your mom have a particular attachment to Lacey?" she asked.

"No, my mom had a special tolerance for Lacey. She never warmed up to her."

For some reason this comment made Cecily feel better. Maybe his mother was one of those overprotective types who thought no woman was good enough for her little boy. Then he continued speaking and dispelled that notion.

"She liked Libby, though. Those two were peas in a pod."

She propped herself up on one elbow and looked down at him. "How long did you and Libby date?"

He opened his eyes and blinked sleepily at her. "A year."

"That's a long time," she said. "Were you serious?"

"Depends on your definition," he said vaguely.

"Tell me yours," she said.

He smiled. "I suppose we were. I proposed."

She would have clutched his shirt, but he wasn't wearing one, so she settled for pressing her palms to his chest. "You what?"

"I proposed. She said no. We broke up. Dobbie came home. End of story."

It was most definitely not the end of the story, at least not for her. Marcus closed his eyes and emitted a soft snore.

"Marcus," she yelled.

His eyes flapped open. "What?"

"You told me you proposed to another woman and then fell asleep."

He smiled. "Honey, it was a lifetime ago. I was a kid."

"It was four years ago. You were two years older than I am now."

"And you're a kid. A beautiful, sexy little kid." He leaned up to kiss her.

"So many things are wrong with that statement, I don't know where to begin," she said.

"Don't try." He kissed her again and shifted her closer.

"Better turn on the radio," she said, and he did.

The next morning she wasn't sure what to expect at breakfast. The elder Henshaws were quiet, but Marcus didn't act like anything was amiss, so she thought maybe they were always quiet in the mornings.

"Mr. Henshaw, would you mind if I brought my horse here?" Cecily asked him.

"Why, no, not at all," Mr. Henshaw said. "You're family now, and there's plenty of room in the barn."

"Thank you." Cecily smiled at him.

"And you can call us Evan and Lydia," he added.

"Thank you," Cecily repeated.

"See you later," Marcus said as soon as he finished eating. He leaned over to kiss her and followed his father from the room.

The silent awkwardness of the table was immediate and oppressive.

"Is there anything I can help you do today, Lydia?" She stumbled over the name. Somehow it was easier to call her Mrs. Henshaw.

"No," Lydia said. "Go stay out of my way." She stood and cleared her plate, despite the fact that her meal was only half finished.

Cecily realized her hands were shaking. She had the sudden desire to flee somewhere and hide. *Home.* The word burned in her brain. She was thankful she had a legitimate reason to go there and hurried through her morning preparations.

When she stepped outside though, she was uncertain of the best way to get there. She didn't feel comfortable taking a truck, and she didn't know where they were kept, anyway. She could take a horse, she knew where the horse barn was, but then how would she get her horse back? Still, that seemed like the best option, so she headed toward the horse barn.

The scent and sounds of the horses worked to calm her troubled heart. She closed her eyes and inhaled deeply.

"I do the same thing," a male voice said. She opened her eyes to see a cowboy watching her with a smile. "Jessup." He held out his hand to her. "I'm the head stable hand here and all around nice guy."

"Cecily Henshaw," she said. She had almost said Blake but corrected herself at the last minute.

He raised an eyebrow at her. "I thought I knew all the Henshaws."

"I'm a new one," she said. She wiggled her ring finger at him.

"Oh my," he said. "Congratulations, Mrs. Henshaw." He grinned and tipped his hat to her.

She smiled. "I would tell you to call me Cecily, but I like hearing my new title too much."

"I'll switch once the newness has worn off for you."

"It's a deal," she said. She glanced wistfully at the horses. "These are some beautiful animals you have."

"Thank you, although I can't take credit for them. I buy, not breed."

"I breed," she said shyly.

"Really?" He perked up interestedly.

She nodded. "My spread is across the way. I was heading there now. I suppose I'll borrow a horse, but I wanted to bring my mare back with me."

"I'll drive you," he offered. "That way I can see what you're up to. We need some fresh horses, and if I can buy locally that's even better."

"I'm not sure I could charge my new father-in-law for horses," she said uncertainly.

"Sure you could. He's loaded. The first rule of business is that everything is business. In fact, if I know Mr. Henshaw, he would probably lose respect for you if you didn't charge him."

"Maybe so," she said. "I guess we'll cross that bridge if we get there." Jessup held out a hand to help her into the truck and ascended into the driver's seat.

"Did you ever think these tall trucks were designed by a lonely man?" he asked.

"No," she said, unsure of his meaning.

"He wanted to think of the easiest way to get his hands on a pretty girl." He grinned at her again.

"Better not share that thought with my husband."

His smile widened. "You like saying that too, huh?"

She nodded.

"Go ahead," he urged.

"Husband, husband, husband," she said, and they laughed together. He was a pleasant man, younger than most of the other hands on the ranch, and personable. They talked about horses for the entire ride, and she was so enthralled by the conversation the drive seemed short.

Back at the ranch Lydia Henshaw was deep in thought. By chance she noticed her pretty new daughter-in-law get in the truck with handsome young Jessup. *There must be some way to use that,* she thought. *Now I have to figure out what it is.*

CHAPTER 14

When they arrived at her ranch, Cecily handed Jessup over to her ranch manager. The two men strolled off, talking horses. Dante was there working hard and she smiled affectionately at him.

He tipped his hat to her. "Mrs. Henshaw," he said coolly.

She crossed her arms over her chest. "I knew you were mad at me."

"Me? Mad? Why would I be mad? Because I didn't get to give my only sister away at her wedding, why would I be angry? By the way, you still haven't told our parents."

"Uh-oh," she said. "I'll tell them tonight. Don't be mad at me, Dante, please? I need you on my side."

"I'm always on your side, Cecily. You took me by surprise. Kitty's in the house, by the way."

"She is?" Cecily perked up. "I didn't see her car."

"She rode her horse."

"Thanks." She took off toward the house at a sprint. "Love you," she threw over her shoulder.

He chuckled. "Love you, too," he yelled.

"Kitty," Cecily blared as soon as she entered the house.

"What?" Kitty said softly. She was sitting on the couch, three feet away.

"I'm glad you're here," Cecily said.

"Me too," Kitty replied. "Dante is working so hard I only see him if I stick around and ride his coattails. I was helping, but I had to use the bathroom."

Cecily smiled. "You don't have to explain to me why you're not working on a ranch that doesn't belong to you."

"How did it go with the in-laws?" Kitty asked. She was observant, and she knew Cecily better than anyone. The lines of strain on her face were obvious.

Cecily's eyes filled with tears. "She hates me."

"Mrs. Henshaw?" Kitty asked incredulously.

Cecily nodded.

"But she's one of the sweetest women I've ever met. I've never even seen her frown."

"That's because you never married one of her sons." She put her hands over her face and pressed her palms against her eyes. "What am I going to do, Kitty? She hates me, I mean really, really hates me. She thinks I trapped Marcus into marriage. She thinks I'm pregnant."

"In nine months she'll see you're not," Kitty said reasonably.

Cecily groaned. "That's the problem. I might be. I didn't think about taking precautions until after it was too late."

"When are you supposed to start your cycle?" Kitty asked.

"I don't know," Cecily said. "You know I've never been regular, so I don't bother keeping track anymore. What am I going to do?" She sank down and rested her head on the back of the couch.

Kitty scooted over and put her arms around her. She wasn't an overly affectionate person, but Cecily was in obvious need of comfort. "We'll figure something out. You can go to town and buy a pregnancy test."

"Our town?" Cecily said incredulously. "Our tiny town where if you stand at one end and sneeze a person at the other end says 'bless you'?"

"You have a point there," Kitty said. She sat up excitedly. "I know;

we'll buy one from the internet. There's an online drug store and everything you buy arrives in a plain brown wrapper. And you can also buy some, um, protection to use in case you're not pregnant."

Cecily narrowed her eyes at her. "How do you know this?" The last she heard Kitty and Dante were also waiting for marriage.

"I read it in a magazine. I've been doing a lot of research. You can never be too prepared."

"That's true," Cecily replied. "Nothing can prepare you for the reality. All right, I'm going to order from here, and I'll have it delivered here, too, in case."

"Now you're thinking like a spy," Kitty said.

"You would know," Cecily said. Kitty was a criminal justice major who dreamed of being in the FBI.

They spent some time on the internet shopping. Cecily ordered a few pregnancy tests because she didn't want to have to order more for a long time. After shopping they went outside and Cecily began working. She said a distracted goodbye to Jessup and thanked him for the ride. It felt good to lose herself in her work again. Her stress and anxiety faded away until she lost track of time and came to with a start.

A frantic glance at her watch showed it was almost suppertime. Cecily had no idea what time the Henshaws ate, but she didn't want to keep them waiting. She said goodbye to Dante, Kitty, and her foreman, saddled her horse, and broke land/speed records to get home.

She paused on the front porch to shake off as much dirt and dust as she could. When she entered the house, three pairs of eyes looked up from the supper table. Marcus smiled, as did his father, but his mother looked annoyed.

"I'm so sorry," Cecily apologized. "I lost track of time, and I forgot to ask what time you eat." She was a grimy mess and wished she had made it home in time to shower. Now she stood back, uncertain if she should change and make them wait, or sit at the table a filthy mess.

"You look like you worked up an appetite," Evan said. "Come sit down."

She flashed him an appreciative smile for the rescue. "Thank you."

She sat, Evan said grace, and they started to eat.

"What did you do today?" Marcus asked.

"I went to my place to work."

"What sort of work do you do?" Evan asked.

"Whatever needs done. Mostly I tend to the horses, but since Dante is home for a few weeks before he starts his new job, he helps do a lot of it. That frees me up to handle the business end of things."

Evan and Marcus gave her amused, indulgent smiles, but didn't comment. Her pride was ruffled, but since they didn't tease her she didn't retort. To them her life might seem like a joke, but she worked hard at what she did, and someday she would have something to show for it.

"Jessup must have enjoyed himself," Lydia said. "He didn't arrive home until a few minutes ago."

"Hmm?" Cecily looked up distractedly. She was still smarting over the looks on the male Henshaws' faces when she talked about her ranch. "I suppose so."

"Jessup was with you all day?" Marcus asked. Something in his tone made Cecily sit up and take notice.

"No. He drove me home and spent some time with my foreman. I can't remember what time he left, but it was awhile ago. He must have gone somewhere else."

"Hmm," Marcus said. Now he looked troubled.

The remainder of the meal was quiet. Cecily thought maybe Lydia mentioned Jessup on purpose. Why did the other woman hate her so much? She had always seemed to like her before the marriage. She always had a kind word when they happened to meet. Surely she couldn't really think Marcus would ever be trapped in a marriage he didn't want. Couldn't she tell her son was happy?

Or was he? Maybe that was the problem. Maybe because Lydia knew him better she could tell he was unhappy when Cecily couldn't. Maybe he was already regretting their hasty marriage and that's why Lydia was being so cool to her. He did look unhappy now as he sat sullenly beside her, picking at his food. As soon as the meal was finished he excused himself and left the house.

"May I help you with the cleanup?" Cecily offered.

"No." Lydia said. She stood and started to clear the table.

"Give her time," Evan said gently. "Mathew's loss was a terrible blow to her. She hasn't been herself lately, and she and Marcus have always been close."

Cecily nodded and tried not to let her expressive face reveal how upset she was. Things were going down the tubes at an alarming rate. "Thank you," she whispered and scurried off to her bedroom before she lost control completely.

She lay on the bed and indulged in a few tears. She always assumed as soon as she turned eighteen her life would magically fall into place. No more would she deal with the uncertainty and emotion of her adolescence. Yet here she was, two years past her eighteenth birthday and still riding an emotional roller coaster. Her father was in prison, her ranch needed constant attention, her husband was angry with her, and she was living with strangers who begrudged her presence. The three days in Las Vegas had been the happiest and best of her life. Now a couple of days later, her happiness was slipping away like sand through her fingers, and she didn't know why.

She didn't hear Marcus enter the room, but there was no mistaking his presence when he lay down beside her and gathered her close to his chest.

"Are you sorry we got married?" he asked.

"No. Are you?"

"No." He smoothed his hand down her hair. "You're young, Lee. You have more oats to sew."

"I don't want oats. I want you."

"Jessup is a womanizer. I don't want you around him."

"I wasn't around him," she said. "He gave me a ride and he wanted to see my horses."

"I don't want you showing another man your horses."

She laughed, but her humor quickly fled. "Your mom hates me."

"No she doesn't," he said. "I'll admit she's having a harder time with the marriage than I thought, but she doesn't hate you. No one could hate you."

She blew out a breath. He would never see the truth, the same way Dante would never believe anything bad about their mother.

"Men," she huffed.

"You got awfully dusty today."

"I worked hard," she said defensively.

"What I meant to say was I think you're in need of a shower."

She sat up, affronted that he would insult her when they hadn't been married a week.

"And so am I," he added.

His meaning started to register. She smiled and kissed him, and they headed for the bathroom together.

CHAPTER 15

The next morning Cecily started her period. She almost cried with relief. The day after that her package from the online drugstore arrived. She stowed the pregnancy tests under the bathroom sink of her house and stuffed her pockets with the birth control she'd purchased. As she was doing that her phone rang. She winced when she recognized the ringtone. It was her father making his weekly phone call from prison.

"Hello, Daddy," she said breathlessly when she answered. She had sprinted to the kitchen to reach her phone.

"Hey, little girl, what are you doing?"

She felt her full pockets and thought it best not to tell him. "Nothing, getting ready to go to work."

"How's our ranch?" She could tell he was smiling and she felt guilty. She had yet to tell him that she had traded out their cows for horses.

"It's good, Dad." Her secrets were piling up on her, and she decided to tell him at least one of them. "Listen, Dad, I don't know quite how to tell you this."

"What?" Alarm rang in his tone.

"I got married."

Dead silence.

"What?" he finally choked.

"I'm married, but don't worry; you know the guy."

"Radley? That nerdy friend of your brother?"

She smiled. "No, someone a little closer to home. I married Marcus Henshaw."

Silence again, and then his hearty laughter rang over the line. "Well, don't that beat all. One of mine marrying into the Henshaws. That's funny. Listen, don't let them take over our land. Henshaws like to acquire, and that ranch is still mine until I die."

"He didn't marry me for my ranch, Dad," she said irritably.

"All the same, you make sure and keep what's ours. I'm not going to let four generations of cattle ranching go down the drain because you fell in love." He paused. "You do love him, don't you?" His tone was softer now, and she smiled.

"Yes, Daddy. I love him very much. He's a wonderful man and a wonderful husband."

"Well that's good. I can't believe your mother didn't tell me this when I talked to her last night."

"Um, I sort of haven't told Mom yet."

Her father blew out a breath. "Cecily, this isn't the kind of secret you can keep from your own mother."

"I haven't been keeping it from her, I've been busy."

"You're never too busy to tell your own mother you got married. I'm going to hang up right now so you can call her." He paused. "I'm sorry I wasn't there for it."

"Me too," she whispered, brushing the tears from her eyes. "But it was nice, nonetheless. I'll send you a picture when we get them back."

"Sounds good. You take care, honey, and make sure that Henshaw treats you right."

"I will, Daddy. I love you."

"I love you too, little one."

They disconnected and she took a deep breath before dialing her mother. She had always been a daddy's girl, and that had caused friction with her mother. Cecily had always felt a little like a pawn between them, and she resented that fact. It wasn't her fault her father favored her, and she didn't understand why her mother acted as if it was.

"Mom," Cecily began.

"What is it?" Her mother's immediate panic probably had more to do with the fact that Cecily never called than it did with anything she read in Cecily's tone.

"Nothing," Cecily said. "I'm calling to talk."

"Oh."

Silence.

"How are you?" Cecily tried.

"Good. Lonely. I miss Dante. I'm used to having him here with me."

But I don't miss you, isn't that what you're trying to say, Mom? She decided to skip the painful small talk and get right to it. "I'm married."

The clunking noise was probably her mother dropping the phone. "You're what?"

"I'm married. I went to Las Vegas and got married a few days ago."

There was silence and then a dial tone.

That went well. Her eyes filled with tears and she dashed them away. Now not only did Marcus's mother hate her, but her own mother did, too.

Once again she threw herself into her work with gusto. A rancher from the other side of town came to inspect her horses and ended up making a large purchase with plans to buy more, but even that good news couldn't lift her flagging spirits.

Marcus noticed her blue mood and downcast eyes at supper, but didn't comment until they were alone in their room.

"What's wrong with you?" he asked. "Did something happen at the ranch?"

"Yes, something very good happened at the ranch today."

"You look happy about it," he said sarcastically.

She gave him a small smile. "I am, but I had a spat with my mother when I called to tell her about us. Not a spat, really, there wasn't time for that. Instead she hung up on me."

His mouth was hanging open in shock.

"That's not so unusual," she explained, taking in his astonishment. "We don't get along the greatest."

He shook his head and pointed to her. While she was talking she had absently emptied her pockets and now he stood staring at the birth control.

"Oh," she said, looking down at the colorful assortment on the bed.

He blinked at her. "Tell me again what it is you do at your ranch."

She giggled. "You stop that." She sat on the bed and motioned for him to join her. "I should have had this discussion with you a few days ago. I'm not on any sort of birth control."

His eyes bugged. "But we…"

"Yes, I know. I was there. I didn't think about it until after. I've been going out of my head with worry, thinking I might be pregnant. But I'm not, so I bought these to use."

"You didn't have to buy those, I have a drawer full."

She crossed her arms over her chest and glared at him.

He winced. "That was probably the wrong thing to tell you."

She continued to stare at him in silence.

"What can I tell you, honey, I wasn't a monk before we got together. I dated my last girlfriend for four years."

She grimaced, not enjoying the reminder of Lacey. "And what about the girls before her? How many have there been?"

He licked his lips nervously. "You really want to know this?"

She nodded.

"There were two other girls, but they weren't serious, and I was always careful."

She studied her fingernails. "Was one of them Libby?"

"No," he said adamantly. "Libby was like you, a good girl. I never would have suggested such a thing to her."

She was more relieved than she could say. She smiled. "Apparently someone did. She's going to have a baby."

"Libby's pregnant?" he exclaimed.

"Yes." She couldn't read his expression. Was it regret? Was he sad the baby wasn't his?

He reached across the bed and laid his hand gently on her stomach. "Were you a little bit sad when you found out you weren't pregnant?"

"A little," she admitted. "But now doesn't seem like a good time." He was staring at her stomach. "Are you disappointed?"

"A little," he admitted.

Was his disappointment because *she* wasn't pregnant with his child, or because Libby wasn't? It was hard to tell, and she hated not knowing.

He smiled. "We have plenty of time to make you that way."

"Do you think your parents are starting to wonder why we play the radio so much?"

He reached for her, and she never got an answer to her question.

CHAPTER 16

For the next couple of weeks Cecily threw herself into work at her ranch. Every morning Jessup was waiting on her to help her with her horse. She tried to do as Marcus wanted and ignore him, but they usually ended up talking horses for a few minutes at the beginning and end of the day.

In the evenings she volunteered to help Lydia with supper or cleanup, but the older woman always refused with a one-word, "No." That was the limit of their communication.

Nightly supper had become a stressful event that usually ended in awkward, oppressive silence. In the beginning Cecily tried to ask questions and make small talk, but Evan was a quiet man by nature and Lydia kept her head down and refused to talk—until one night when she couldn't seem to stop talking.

"Remember, Marcus, when you and Libby used to go out riding some nights after supper," she said.

Marcus looked at her in confusion because she said it randomly and out of the blue.

"Yes," he said.

"Those were good times," she commented.

"Uh, huh," he agreed, still sounding wary and uncertain. He looked at Cecily out of the corner of his eye. "Cecily is amazing on a horse. She probably could have gone pro, although now it's too late. I don't want her around all those other men." He winked at her and smiled.

Her happiness was short-lived when Lydia continued. "Libby was such a helpful, sweet girl. She always worked in the kitchen with me to make supper, and there wasn't a night she was here that she didn't help clean up."

Cecily's cheeks flamed with the injustice of it all. She had offered to help every night since her arrival, but she had been rebuffed. Now Lydia was making it sound like she was content to sit on her laurels and be waited on. If she tried to defend herself she would come off looking like an oversensitive nut job because there had been no blatant accusation.

"Libby likes working in the kitchen, Mom," Marcus said.

"Some girls aren't cut out for domesticity, I guess," Lydia said.

But I do like to work in the kitchen, Cecily wanted to say. *I do like to cook and clean, I have other priorities right now.*

"Jessup tells me you've been doing some horse breeding over at that ranch of yours," Evan said. She thought he probably said it to rescue her by turning the topic to a safe one, but it had the opposite effect.

"Jessup?" Marcus inserted. "What does he know about it?"

"Quite a lot," Evan blustered on, totally oblivious to the tension he was creating. "I've never had much taste for horse breeding, but I can see how we need something like that in these parts. Jessup asked if he might be allowed to help out at your place. I told him yes."

"Thank you." Cecily forced the words past stiff lips. Her dear, sweet father-in-law had no idea how much he had complicated her life, but her mother-in-law did. She was now smiling pleasantly as she heaped another helping of potatoes on Marcus's plate.

Marcus was now sitting stiff and silent beside her.

I have got to get out of this house, Cecily thought. She offered to help Lydia clean up and practically ran away when the woman gave her a scathing look and shook her head.

She sprinted to the one place of solace that always brought her comfort—her horse. Thankfully Jessup was nowhere around, so she saddled her horse for herself and took off at breakneck speed.

After a half an hour of hard riding she slowed her horse to a walk and let him amble along a pretty stream. The pastoral scene had a soothing effect on her frayed emotions.

The problem was that everything was out of her control. She couldn't control how Lydia felt about her. She couldn't control Marcus's unfounded jealousy. She could control her actions and reactions, but so far she didn't think she was doing anything wrong.

She hopped off her horse, picked up a rock, and skipped it in the stream.

"It's not fair," she raged out loud.

"What's not?"

She jumped and spun to look at Marcus.

"Everything," she said.

He slipped off his horse and came to stand beside her. He picked up a rock to skip. "This reminds me of that day in the stream, acting like kids. Except now we're doing it with our emotions."

She put her hands on her hips. "Are you calling me immature?"

"Yes, but I'm including myself in that description. I'm acting like a jealous teenager."

She waited for him to continue to criticize himself, but instead he turned on her. "And you're acting the same way over Libby, a woman who is happily married and lives far away."

"An hour is not far away," she contradicted.

He stared at her without reply. He had to see how his mother was fueling the situation, didn't he? How could she stand to hear herself being compared to Libby, a paragon of virtue in his mother's eyes?

Finally a smile tugged at the corner of his mouth. She was beginning to know that look, so she wasn't surprised when he strode over and wrapped his arms tightly around her.

"Let's compromise and say I am acting immature and jealous over Jessup, and you're acting immature and jealous over Libby." He leaned close and pressed his lips to her neck.

"You're six years older. You should be better behaved," she said weakly. She couldn't resist him when he kissed her neck, and he knew it. After only a few weeks of marriage, he had learned her weakness and routinely used it against her.

He laughed and the vibration tickled. "You don't give an inch do you, Mrs. Henshaw?"

Hearing her name on his lips made her already weak knees weaker. "I might be persuaded."

He pulled her closer, but she stilled his hands.

"I didn't bring anything from the drawer."

"I think we're all right," he said. "This once. We'll be careful from now on."

She studied him, uncertainly. Finally she smiled. "See? I do occasionally give in to you," she said, and then she put her face up to be kissed.

The sun was starting to set as they lay by the stream, arm in arm.

"We should go," he said.

She groaned.

He smiled. "I have to say, it was nice not to have to use the radio."

"We wouldn't have to use it ever again if we moved to my house," she said.

"I know it's difficult on you to live with my parents, Lee. All I'm asking is that you're patient for a little while longer. Let me give them time to heal from Mathew's death and adjust to our marriage and then we'll find a place of our own. Besides, think of the rent we're saving." He poked her waist.

"This must be how the Henshaws got their wealth. They're all skinflints." She rolled away and sprang up when he came after her.

"For that I'm going to tell you what I came out to tell you in the first place before you distracted me," he said.

"What?" she asked. She allowed him to catch her and clasped her arms around his neck.

"Your mother called after you left the house," he said. "She's coming for a visit."

She gasped, placed her hands over her mouth, and would have fallen over if he didn't catch her.

"Lee, what's the big deal? It's only your mom."

"That's like saying it's only a hurricane. You don't understand."

"Then explain it to me."

"She doesn't like me."

"Of course she does," he said.

"Marcus, will you please stop saying that when I tell you people don't like me? I know who does and doesn't like me."

"Sure you do, baby," he said patronizingly. "Why do you believe your own mother, your flesh and blood, doesn't like you?"

"Because my father does," she said. She sat on the bank once again and plucked a long blade of grass. "My dad has always favored me since my birth. He used to be horrible to Dante; it was what caused my parents' divorce. But the way he doted on me added to it."

He sat down across from her and took her hand. "You think she's jealous of you because you had the brunt of your father's attention," he said.

She nodded.

"I suppose that makes sense," he said. "But here's the good news: I'm right here."

She looked at him in wonder. It had honestly never occurred to her that he would help her face her mother. "You're my husband," she murmured, a bit of awe in her tone.

"Last time I checked," he said dryly. "We're partners, in every way."

Her answering smile was jubilant. "And I thought you were here only for my physical enjoyment. This is like sprinkles on ice cream." She pulled him close and kissed him, and then they hopped on their horses and rode home.

CHAPTER 17

Cecily spent the next two days obsessively cleaning her ranch house. Her mother hadn't visited in two years, since her father's incarceration when the family had figuratively circled their wagons. It was the closest the two women ever came to having a real relationship. Most of the time they stayed out of each other's way.

She thought for certain she wouldn't be able to sleep the night before the visit, but she slept soundly and woke refreshed. After the initial adjustment of sleeping next to Marcus, she now slept better beside him and wondered how she had slept alone for so many years without his arm curled protectively around her.

"Today's the day," he murmured sleepily against her ear.

She groaned. "Thank you for the reminder."

He smiled. "Sarcasm doesn't suit you, Babe."

"It had better learn to adjust; I can't live without it," she said.

"Strange, I say the same thing about you," he returned. "I hate to rush, but I have to. Lots to do today."

She groaned again. "You own the ranch. Can't you take the occasional day off?"

"I will when you do," he said. He had commented a few times on how hard she worked her ranch. He always said it with pride. She was too embarrassed to tell him part of the reason she threw herself into her work was to escape his mother.

She rolled over to face him and pressed her palm to his cheek. "Let's take a second honeymoon. Right now. This minute. We can go anywhere you want."

"You can't run away from your mother; she'll always find you."

So will yours, she thought bitterly. He kissed her and some of her tension eased, only to reappear with more strength after he left for the day. She ate a hurried, stressful breakfast with his mother and then, after offering to clean up and being rebuffed, exited the house with expediency.

"Hello, Jessup," she called, hurriedly ascending into the saddle before he could start a conversation. She felt nervous and jittery and riding her horse didn't work to calm her as it usually did. She wished Dante was still home to run interference like usual, but he had moved to Omaha to start his new job as an actuary, and Kitty went with him to help him settle in to the city. She attended the University of Nebraska there, and was familiar with all the place had to offer.

Her mother declined her offer to pick her up in town, saying she would make her own way to the ranch, and Cecily was not-so-secretly relieved. It was torture to have to wait around for her mother to show up, but it would have been worse if they had to make awkward small talk on the hour-long drive from town.

Instead of working outside like she normally did, she worked in the kitchen preparing supper. Lydia Henshaw hadn't uttered a word about inviting Shelby Blake for supper, so Cecily took matters into her own hands. She was cooking dinner for everyone at her own house and inviting her in-laws there. After careful thought she decided to make Spanish food. She hoped it would make her mother happy and her in-laws impressed, so she was now preparing a menu of various tapas and paella along with a caramel flan for dessert.

The front door slammed and she winced. She was only partway through with her meal preparation; how could time have slipped away so quickly?

"Smells good in here," Marcus said. She whirled to face him with a look of delight.

"Marcus," she said dumbly. She wondered if he was imaginary.

He grinned. "Surprise."

"What are you doing here?"

"I came to see my girl. I thought about what you said this morning, and you're right. I should take the day off to spend with you and your moth…"

His words were cut off when she ran across the room, leapt into his arms and kissed him soundly.

"I take it you approve." He could barely get the words out because she was pelting his face with kisses.

"I love you," she said when her ardor cooled slightly. He smiled indulgently at her. "I mean it, Marcus. I really and truly love you." She cupped his face and kissed him again, tenderly this time. The kiss was starting to spiral out of control when she heard her mother's voice behind them.

"Something's burning in here and I don't think it's the food."

Cecily reluctantly let go of him, noting as she did so his cheeks were tinged a faint pink. She smiled. She had never seen him blush before. Her mother had caught her kissing boys, but having his mother-in-law catch him locked in a passionate embrace was new for Marcus.

He set Cecily down. She took his hand and turned him to her mother.

"Mom, you remember Marcus. Marcus, this is my mother, Shelby Blake."

"Diaz-Blake," Shelby corrected. "But you can call me Shelby."

"Shelby," Marcus said warmly. He held out his hand and they shook. "It's nice to see you again."

She nodded. "You were only eighteen when I left," she said.

"I was only twelve," Cecily said. She darted a mischievous glance at Marcus.

He put her in a headlock. "Yes, please remind your mother of my cradle-robbing tendencies." He kissed her cheek.

"It's not the cradle-robbing that bothers me so much as the speed with which you did it," Shelby said.

"Mom," Cecily bristled. *Ten seconds before she started in on me. A new record*, she thought.

Shelby held up her hands in supplication. "All I'm saying is that a little warning would have been nice, Cecily. Or an invitation to your wedding."

"I'm afraid that's my fault," Marcus tried.

Shelby brushed his words aside as if he hadn't spoken. "I've never known any of your family to be impulsive, Marcus. My daughter, on the other hand." She let the insinuation hang.

Cecily clenched her hands into fists. "Mother, I am twenty years old. If I want to get married on the spur of the moment then that's my business."

"Yes, because it worked out so well for your father and me," Shelby said acidly.

"And I suppose that's my fault, too," Cecily yelled. "Besides, you and Dad are back together, aren't you?"

"As back together as we can be when one of us is in prison," Shelby said.

"What's that supposed to mean?" Cecily said. "That Marcus is doomed to end up in prison because we married quickly?"

Marcus cleared his throat. "Can I help you with supper, honey?" he asked, and gave Cecily a pointed look. She took a deep breath and tried to calm down.

"That would be great," she said. "Why don't you help Mom with her bags first?" She smiled at him and realized as she did so what a soothing balm it was to have him nearby.

He smiled at Cecily and winked as he passed her. "Come on, Shelby, you can tell me embarrassing stories about Cecily when she was little."

"I'm sure you know a few of them," Shelby said. "You watched her grow up, after all."

Cecily opened her mouth to retort but stopped when Marcus turned around and shook his head at her. Instead she stuck her tongue out at him and he chuckled.

"I am clearly delusional and in need of mental help," Cecily whispered to Marcus when her mother left the kitchen to use the bathroom. "Why I thought cooking Spanish food would be a good idea is anybody's guess."

She had forgotten the way it was when her mother was teaching her to cook the food of their heritage; all the screaming, fighting, and arguing that ensued. Instead she had conjured a rosy image of mother/daughter bonding that in no way resembled reality.

"Too much saffron and not enough chorizo," were her mother's first words as soon as she entered the kitchen after unloading her bags.

"How do you know that when you haven't even tasted it?" Cecily asked.

"I can smell, can't I? And I've been cooking it longer than you."

"And making it so spicy no one can bear to eat it," Cecily said. "I'm leaving out some of the chorizo because Marcus's parents don't like spicy things."

"Everyone likes spicy things," Shelby said.

Cecily sighed in frustration. The worst part of their relationship was that Shelby was normal with everyone else. She doted on Kitty and never had an unkind word for her. With everyone else she was sweet, kind, loving and supportive. It was only with Cecily that her claws came out, and Cecily could seemingly do nothing right.

"Mother, when you make the paella you can make it exactly how you like. When I'm making it in my home I will make it the way I like it."

Shelby raised an eyebrow at her. "This isn't my home anymore?"

"You haven't lived in it for eight years," Cecily said.

"Legally I still own it," Shelby said.

Cecily put her hands on her hips. "You do not. You lost it in the divorce."

Shelby had forgotten that fact. "Throw that up in my face, why don't you?"

"I'm not throwing anything up in your face, Mother; I'm merely pointing out that you do not, in fact, own this house."

Shelby cast about for something to say but Marcus preempted her before she could find it.

"You two look remarkably alike. It's almost like Yancey contributed no genes of his own," he said. Both women had long black hair, dark complexions, and dark eyes, although Shelby was obviously older with a slightly darker complexion.

"She certainly received her father's stubbornness," Shelby said.

"He says I got it from you," Cecily returned.

"Our kids will get it from my side, too," Marcus said. "They don't have much chance of being docile."

Shelby looked up at him in shock and then turned her attention to Cecily. "You're pregnant. I knew it."

"I am not," Cecily said hotly.

"And that's why you're leaving the chorizo out. I couldn't eat spicy things when I was pregnant, either."

Cecily looked at her and dumped a handful of chorizo in the paella. "Not pregnant," she said.

Shelby eyed her critically. "Don't lie to me. I can tell you've gained weight."

Cecily's mouth fell open. Beside her Marcus tried his hardest to stifle a laugh. He didn't succeed. She smacked him in the stomach with the back of her hand before turning on her mother.

"I am not pregnant, and I have not gained weight. If anything I've lost weight." She stirred the paella, tasted it and frowned harder. It was too spicy now.

"I guess time will tell," Shelby said resignedly.

Cecily threw down her spoon. "I'll go take a pregnancy test right now if you want, Mom. In fact, you can come watch me so you're sure I don't use someone else's urine to fake it."

"There's no need for melodrama," Shelby said.

"I think there is because it seems to be all you understand," Cecily said.

"Then please explain to me how this marriage came about," Shelby said. "I asked Dante and Kitty and neither of them knew you were even dating."

"We weren't," Cecily admitted.

"Then why did you get married?" Shelby asked.

She blushed as she thought of Marcus's reason for the marriage. She couldn't very well tell her mother that the only reason he married her was because she believed in saving herself for marriage. At least she could tell her the reason she married him.

"Because I fell in love with him, all right?" Cecily said impatiently. "Because he makes me feel like no one else and I can't live without him. I'm sorry if it didn't fit your timetable, and I truly am sorry you weren't at the wedding, especially because it was beautiful and perfect, but you haven't had to live in this small community after Dad went to prison. You got to be anonymous in Chicago. You haven't had to deal with people whispering about you behind your back or saying horrible things to your face. I didn't want to have a long engagement or public wedding where people would feel sorry for Marcus for being tied down to poor Cecily Blake whose father is a criminal. I wanted to go away with him and steal a few days of happiness for the two of us before coming back here and facing everything and everyone waiting to make sure our happiness doesn't last." Somewhere during the course of her speech she started to cry.

Tears streamed down her face and she didn't bother to wipe them away.

"Come here," Marcus commanded gently. He put his arm around her waist and ushered her into the living room. He sat on the couch, settled her in his lap and murmured gentle, soothing words to her until her tears stopped.

"Now do you see why I wanted to go away?" she asked when her tears dimmed enough for her to speak.

He smiled at her and smoothed her hair off her face. "I see that and your mother are alike. It's like steel on steel. She loves you; she doesn't know how to communicate with you. We'll work on that." He hugged her. "You're doing great, and supper smells amazing. I didn't know you could cook."

She pressed her face to his neck. "I love you, Marcus."

He tipped her face up to his and kissed her. "Ready to go back?" he asked.

"I suppose so," she said. She reluctantly eased out of his embrace and followed him back to the kitchen.

If she had any delusions that her tears would have a softening effect on her mother, she was sadly mistaken. The older woman stood at the stove, wooden spoon in hand.

"I fixed the paella for you. It's edible now," her mother said.

Cecily turned from the room, fled the house, went to her horse, and rode away.

CHAPTER 19

It took a long time for Marcus to coax Cecily back to the house. The only way he succeeded was by reminding her that his parents were coming to supper soon and she had tapas in the oven.

She actually smiled at that. "You've never said the word 'tapas' in your life, have you?"

He returned her smile and brushed his knuckles along her jaw. "I'm having a lot of firsts with you."

She would love to stay and find out what that meant, but he was right; there was work to be done. When they returned to the house, he adeptly ushered her mother out of the kitchen and kept her in the living room talking until his parents arrived.

Cecily went out to greet them, wiping her hands on the dishtowel tucked in her jeans. Her mother and the Henshaws were already deep in friendly-looking conversation. Once again she noticed how both her mother and Lydia Henshaw were the soul of polite perfection to anyone but her. Her opinion was reinforced when both women turned to her with disapproving scowls.

"So you do know your way around a kitchen," Lydia said.

"Do you realize you have a dishtowel in your pants?" her mother asked.

She looked to Marcus for moral support. He winked and mouthed, "Sexy," and she turned and went back into the kitchen with a smile.

They ate in the kitchen. Their house was smaller and more casual than the Henshaw's. Cecily had never minded before, but she saw it now with fresh eyes as she thought of the Henshaw's grand dining room where they took most meals.

This is who I am, she repeated to herself over and over. *I'm a country girl who makes paella. There's nothing wrong with that.*

She had to repeat it often as she surreptitiously watched her mother-in-law's face. The older woman looked around at the well-worn oak furniture in barely concealed distaste.

"Is this paella?" she asked when Cecily set a bowl of the colorful stew in front of her.

"Yes it is," Cecily said happily, determined to stay positive.

"I'm allergic to shellfish," she said, and pushed the bowl away.

"Since when?" Marcus asked.

"Since always. You probably don't know because we don't get much of it here in the middle of Montana. I'm almost certain you were there when I told Libby. Of course, she usually cooked regional dishes."

"This is a regional dish in our family," Shelby said. Was that protectiveness Cecily heard in her tone, or was she imagining things? "My parents are from Spain. Cecily has been eating paella since she had teeth."

Cecily forced a smile at Lydia. "There are plenty of tapas, and none of them has shellfish," she said.

"Tapas?" Lydia repeated the word like it was a disease.

"That's a fancy Spanish word for appetizers," Marcus said. "I bet you had no idea Cecily was so diverse, or so talented." He gave a pointed and warning glance to his mother.

"No, I had no idea," she said dully.

"What does Yancey think of all the changes Cecily is making to his ranch?" Evan asked. "I hardly recognized the place." Once again her kind father-in-law's attempt to rescue her was about to make things much, much worse.

"Changes?" Shelby echoed. She looked at her daughter in question.

Cecily cleared her throat. "I've been phasing out cattle and breeding horses instead."

"Your father didn't mention it," Shelby said.

"He doesn't exactly know." She fiddled with her napkin. Paper napkin, she thought absently. The Henshaws always used cloth napkins.

"You've been keeping secrets from your father?" Shelby asked. By her tone Cecily couldn't tell if it was disapproving or not.

She started to shred the napkin. "Well, Dad's not here, Mom," she said slowly. "I wasn't doing well with the cattle business. I know nothing about cows. I know lots about horses, and I enjoy them. I had to make the switch or lose the ranch." She repressed a shudder with the memory of how close she had come to losing everything. "The horses are starting to turn a profit, and I think it's going to be quite lucrative after I'm well established."

"That's so," Evan agreed. "I've had Jessup looking into things."

She fought a frown. She loved her new father-in-law, but this was her business.

"Dad, you should have asked Cecily's permission for that," Marcus said.

"He was trying to be helpful," Lydia said. "Surely she has enough sense to recognize she needs help to make this ranch livable. Although I suppose she recognized that before the marriage."

"Mother," Marcus said. He looked at his mother as if he had never seen her before, and he probably hadn't. She had never said anything so blatantly critical in his presence before, although she had said that much and worse to Cecily in private. "Let me clear something up once and for all. Lee didn't pursue me, I pursued her. I married her because I wanted to, not because I had to, and not because she tricked me into it."

Lydia looked unconvinced.

Evan cleared his throat. "I do apologize if I overstepped my bounds, Cecily. I can't seem to help from taking on a challenge in the business world, and your operation here intrigues me."

She studied him, realizing she was being oversensitive. And by all accounts he was a business genius. Perhaps she had been too short-sighted in trying to keep him out of everything when it was obvious she could benefit from his help. Impulsively she stood to give him a tight hug.

"No, I'm the one who is sorry, Evan. I do appreciate your help here. I suppose I'm sensitive because I've been doing it all myself, and my pride wants to succeed or fail on my own merit, but that's not a reasonable way to run a business."

He cleared his throat, embarrassed but pleased by her display. "Yes, well, you're family now." He took a bite of the paella. "This is good."

"Thank you." She smiled at him. Her eyes fell on Marcus. He was beaming at her with pride and affection. But when her eyes settled on Lydia, her smile died. The woman was looking at her with smoldering resentment, and she knew if she hated her before it was nothing compared to what she felt now. In her mother-in-law's mind she had crossed over the line by winning Evan to her side. Cecily knew this because it was the same look her mother gave her every time her father had fawned affectionately over her.

The story of my life, Cecily thought. *My fathers love me, and my mothers hate me.*

"How long are you able to stay, Shelby?" Marcus asked. She couldn't tell what Marcus's opinion of her mother was, and she wondered if his real question was, "How soon can I get rid of you?"

Shelby must have wondered the same thing because her smile was wry. "I'm staying a few days here and then going to Omaha to visit Dante and Kitty."

"Are they engaged yet?" Lydia asked. Her smile looked sweet and sentimental, much more like the woman Cecily knew before her marriage.

"Not yet, but any day now. Between you, me, and the wall, Dante spent a lot of time ring shopping last time he was in Chicago."

"He didn't tell me that," Cecily said, affronted by being kept out of the loop.

"My children like secrets, apparently," Shelby said, scowling at Cecily as she ate another bite of paella.

"He's a lucky boy," Lydia said. "Kitty's such a sweet girl. All the Chapman girls are." She swallowed hard. Mathew had been very briefly engaged to Maggie Chapman before his death.

Cecily swallowed hard, too, but her emotions had more to do with wistfulness. She wished her mother-in-law would talk about her that way and sigh with happiness over her marriage to her son.

"Kitty feels like a daughter to me already," Shelby said. "She and Cecily have always been close, and she spent so many nights here when they were little girls."

She spent a lot of nights here after that, too, but you were in Chicago with Dante, Cecily thought, and was surprised by her own bitterness. She had no idea she resented her mother for leaving and taking her brother.

"Will you be returning to the ranch after Yancey's release?" Marcus asked.

"Marcus, that's a personal question that's none of your business," Lydia chided, but she looked interested in the answer all the same.

Shelby smiled. "It's all right. I'm sure everyone is confused and curious over our convoluted family situation. To tell you the truth, I don't want to come back here. Too many ghosts, if you know what I mean. I've made a life for myself in Chicago, and I'm hoping Yancey might join me there."

Cecily was instantly defensive. "But Dad loves the ranch. He's lived here his whole life and he doesn't know anything else."

Shelby's irritation was immediate, too. "Cecily, he'll be almost seventy years old when he's released. That's a reasonable time to retire."

"But," Cecily started again, but Marcus caught her eye and shook his head. She almost wanted to cry over the thought of her father not returning to the ranch, but then she thought about it from her mother's point of view. She never adapted to ranch life, even when she was happy with her father. She was a city girl. Cecily looked at Marcus again. If for some reason she decided to leave the ranch and go somewhere else, wouldn't she hope that he would follow? She would follow him, no matter where he went. She took a breath. "Maybe that would be for the best. The ranch might have too many painful memories for Dad, too. Besides, I think he would like Chicago if he gave it a chance. I liked it there. I almost didn't come home."

Marcus scowled at her.

"I didn't know you then," she said. "Obviously if I had you here waiting for me nothing would have kept me away." She covered his hand with hers and squeezed. He smiled and when she happened to glance at her mother she was smiling, too. There was something Cecily didn't recognize in her look, and she realized with a start that it was approval.

"Maybe you could put a bug in your dad's ear about Chicago," her mother said. "He listens to you, and I think if we start working on him now he might be ready when he gets out in eight years."

"Maybe I will," Cecily said. She and her mother shared a smile, and she tucked into her paella with gusto.

CHAPTER 20

"*L*ydia doesn't like you."

"Be blunt, Mom, don't spare my feelings."

"I never do."

They were cleaning the kitchen together after Lydia, Evan, and Marcus went home.

"She hates me. I've tried to be nice to her, honestly I have, Mom, but nothing works. Marcus doesn't see it at all."

"I think he did tonight," Shelby said. "But that's not surprising. Your father thought his mother walked on water. It's the way with men, and it was one of many issues between your father and me."

"I don't want it to be an issue between me and Marcus, but I don't see any solution."

"You could move out and live here," Shelby suggested.

"Marcus doesn't feel like he can leave his parents so soon after Mathew's death."

"Marcus needs to grow up and put his wife before his parents," Shelby said with no small amount of venom.

"Mom," Cecily said uncomfortably. It was nice to have her mother on her side, but she was uncomfortable with her criticism of Marcus.

Shelby expelled a breath. "Sorry. I suppose your marriage is bringing up a lot of issues from my marriage. I know you think I'm a critical shrew out to ruin your life, but the truth is that I'm worried about you. I don't want you to make the same mistakes I did. I know you feel very in love with Marcus right now, and I'll admit he's a very nice man, but you can't live on love forever. Feelings fade. Marriage is hard."

"Mom, I don't want to hear this right now. I've only been married a few weeks."

"This is exactly when you need to hear it, Cecily. Marriage is forever. You can't take the same path your dad and I did and run away when things don't work out. I thought I was doing what was best for Dante to protect him. Then your Dad went off the deep end, and Dante ended up getting sucked into his life anyway, and I wasn't there for you the way I should have been. I hated the feeling of having to choose between you."

"You chose Dante," Cecily said softly. There. It was out. The issue she had been holding against her mother for eight years.

"I chose the child I thought needed me most. You were strong and independent and you had your father's adoration. Dante was insecure and had his father's contempt. It never meant I didn't love you, or that it wasn't agonizing to leave you, but you wouldn't have come with me, and you know it."

"I wouldn't have," Cecily admitted. She had adored her father and the ranch. "But you could have asked."

"I could have. I should have. But this is what I'm talking about, honey. Age brings wisdom. Hindsight is twenty-twenty. You are making decisions right now that will affect your life and your future. I want you to choose wisely. I don't want you to get hurt."

Cecily was quiet as she thought that over. "Mom, all I can do is try to make good decisions, but I have to make my own mistakes."

Shelby smiled. "I guess we are a lot alike. I said the same thing to my mom."

Cecily fiddled with the dishtowel in her hand. "Your life wasn't horrible, was it, Mom?"

"Of course not. Leaving you and your dad was terrible, but it was one small part of a good life. A great life, with great kids I love very much."

"And Dad. You love Dad, don't you?"

Shelby pulled her close and hugged her. "It's important to you that I love your dad, isn't it?"

Cecily nodded and swiped at her tears. She needed her parents to love each other on a number of different levels—as their child who dreamed of her parents being happy, and as a woman who desperately needed them as a positive example.

"Yes, honey. I love your father, with all his faults and insecurities. I love him completely, always and forever. I've never loved anyone else. And I'll tell you a secret, one woman to another. I've never touched another man in my entire life. There's only always been your father, and there will always only be him."

Cecily wiped her eyes again. "Thanks for telling me, Mom." She hesitated, unwilling to trod on the sudden bond between them, but needing to ask more questions. "Do you have any advice for me about my mother-in-law?"

"You could do what I did," her mother said ruefully. "You could bottle it all up, try to stuff down your resentment, and then fly off the handle and tell her every negative thing she ever did to you."

"You did that to Grandma?" Cecily asked. She didn't know her grandmother; she had died before Cecily was born.

Shelby nodded. "It was a huge mistake. It did nothing but make the alienation between us worse, and your father was livid with me. When I finally softened my heart enough to realize I needed to make amends, she dropped dead of a heart attack." She twisted the sponge in her hand, unaware that some water leaked out. "Your father never came out and said it, but I think he blamed me in some way for her death. That's why when he wanted to name you after her I didn't protest. It's also one of the reasons he doted on you so much. You were a reminder of the mother he lost."

Cecily saw the pattern with her parents and didn't want to repeat it. "I guess I won't try that way."

"Better not," Shelby said. She reached out and squeezed Cecily's hand. "The Lydia I saw tonight isn't the Lydia I've known for almost thirty years. Try and make an allowance for Mathew's death. If I lost one of you I would go insane. Give her some time, breathing room, and patience. She'll come around sooner or later, honey. You're sort of irresistible. Like your mother."

They shared another smile. Cecily wondered at the magic between them tonight. She wasn't sure if it was because she was married, or because she was allowing her marriage to mature her in ways she never knew she needed.

Shelby hugged her tightly and kissed her cheek. "I'll finish cleaning the kitchen. Go home to your husband, little girl."

It was dark by the time she saddled her horse. She hadn't thought about the fact that she'd brought her horse when she sent Marcus home without her. He hadn't either because he would never let her ride home alone in the dark, especially not with Mathew's killer still roaming free. She rode nervously, warily, all the way home and was relieved Marcus wasn't waiting outside for her. He probably would have given her an earful if he realized.

He was barely half awake when she reached their bedroom. She changed her clothes and settled in beside him.

"Dinner was good," he said. He slung his arm over her waist and squeezed gently.

"Thank you. Do you like my mother?"

"I've only been married a few weeks, but I know better than to walk into that minefield."

"It's not a loaded question. I'm curious, is all."

"I like her fine so long as she doesn't pick on you." He pulled her close and kissed the rim of her ear.

She smiled. The day had been long and exhaustion was creeping in. "Marcus, I love you," she murmured sleepily.

He propped himself up on one elbow to look down at her. He traced the outline of her face, not sure why he should feel shy about admitting his feelings to her. She was his wife, after all. He waited until he was sure she was asleep before he spoke.

"I love you too, Lee." He kissed her cheek and leaned across her to turn out the light.

CHAPTER 21

The next couple of days with her mother were the best they ever spent together, at least as far as Cecily could remember. They butted heads, but gently and affectionately. Cecily hoped it would last and be the new order of things, but she had twenty years of experience to make her wary. Still, she was sad to see her mother go, if only for the excuse it provided her to be away from the Henshaw house. She and Marcus had dined at the ranch with her mother for the past two nights, and it was heavenly to have a break from the constant stress.

After her mother left, the tension at the Henshaw's notched up to a fever pitch, and it was starting to take a toll on Cecily. She threw herself into her ranch with more fervor and fell into bed exhausted each night. Marcus noticed and complained.

"Lee, you're pushing yourself too hard."

"No harder than you push yourself," she returned. His busyness was becoming a source of contention between them, as were her frequent trips to her ranch. "If you worked on Wall Street people would call you a workaholic, but because you own the ranch they say you're dedicated."

They glared at each other in a tense standoff. Part of the problem was the fact that they were too tired even for anything more than a hurried goodnight kiss lately, and the physical distance was making them irritable.

"We've been married six weeks and you're already too tired to be with me," he said.

"And you're already too busy to be with me," she said.

They went to bed angry for the first time in their short marriage, but she couldn't sleep. He was out like a light, which notched up her anger until it turned to hurt. Finally her pathetic weeping woke him and they spent a long time making up.

But other factors were wearing on their relationship, too, namely his mother. Her insults and barbs to Cecily were getting more frequent and more pointed. Most of them concerned Libby Dobbins.

"Libby stopped by," she said one day. "They have an abundance of peaches this year and she baked us a pie. I'm sure she remembers that's Marcus's favorite. She was always baking him things. He likes a girl who can bake. Most men do."

Marcus made it worse later that night by his headlong reaction to the pie.

"Mom, you outdid yourself," he said. "This is the best pie I've ever had. You know how much I love peach."

Lydia smiled gleefully. "I didn't make it. Libby did. She brought it over today. Such a sweet girl, isn't she? You two were happy together."

His hand froze with his fork halfway to his mouth. "Not as happy as she and Dobbie are together," he said.

What was that in his tone? Regret? Jealousy?

Exasperation would be a more apt term, but she didn't know because Marcus didn't tell her. He had no idea his mother held Libby over Cecily's head on an almost daily basis, but he did wonder why she wouldn't let the past lie. He and Libby hadn't dated for years now, and they were both married to other people.

But to Cecily, who was already sensitized to any mention of his former girlfriend, his silence and frown looked like sadness over the one who got away. She didn't point out that she was also an excellent baker. There was no need. She swore she would never make a peach pie again as long as she lived. In fact, she had no appetite for one now.

"Excuse me," she murmured, and then set aside her fork and pushed back from the table.

"I guess I'll do the dishes alone. Again," Lydia said.

Her husband frowned at her. He had heard Cecily offer to help her every night since her arrival, but Marcus hadn't. Strangely his wife waited to rebuff Cecily's offers of help until Marcus was out of earshot. He shook his head. He would never understand women. He was glad he'd had sons.

Marcus was frowning, too. He wondered why Cecily didn't offer to help. He hated to think of his poor mother doing all the domestic work herself, especially when Cecily was adding more work simply by being an extra mouth to feed, launder, and clean up after.

When he reached the bedroom and found Cecily lying down asleep his anger boiled over.

"Cecily, this is ridiculous. It's not even seven at night."

She jumped awake and lay still as a wave of dizziness assaulted her. "I didn't mean to fall asleep," she murmured. She had only closed her eyes for a minute, or so she thought.

He came to sit at the edge of the bed. "You're working too hard if you fall asleep like this and steal away to our room without even offering to help clean up." He had always imagined whoever he married helping in the kitchen with his mother. The fact that Cecily didn't was a disappointment to him.

She sat up slowly and her mouth opened. "You have got to be kidding me."

"No, I'm not."

"I have offered to help until I'm blue in the face. She won't let me."

His frown deepened. "That doesn't make any sense. Why wouldn't she want help? She said she did. I'm sure she gets tired of doing all the work herself."

Her eyes filled with tears. That tugged at his heart, but he was too angry to be dissuaded from his purpose. "Why do you think? She wants to make me look bad in your eyes."

He ran a hand through his hair. "Cecily, that's ridiculous. You're making her sound as cold-blooded as Hitler."

"You always take her side," Cecily said. She dashed at her tears. "You don't see what she's doing to me, to us."

"What? What is she doing to us? We're still married, still together. That hasn't changed, and it won't." Despite his anger he needed to be clear on that point.

Her tears spilled over and ran unchecked down her cheeks. She wasn't sure why she was crying so violently, she just was. He started to soften toward her until she continued.

"People aren't meant to live with their parents this way," she said. "Don't you get it? It's her house. I have nothing of my own here. I'm an intruder, and she makes sure I know it at every turn. And you do nothing to back me up. You won't listen to me. You refuse to see how she's treating me."

Some of her words resonated as truth, and that made him angry. He wasn't ready to admit defeat where his parents were concerned. They needed him now to see them through Mathew's loss.

"What I see is her feeding you, cooking for you, cleaning up after you, and doing your laundry. All without any help on your part while you nap and pout like a little girl."

He went too far and he knew it when her eyes grew round and wounded, but his pride wouldn't let him take anything back.

"I guess you would see it that way," she said listlessly. She gathered her clothes and went into the bathroom to take a long shower. When she exited the bathroom he was outside. She crawled into bed, too hurt and too tired to do anything but fall asleep.

CHAPTER 22

They didn't speak or touch for three days. The worst part for Cecily was seeing the gleeful, delighted look on Lydia's face. Her only consolation was that Evan watched them with quiet concern, and Marcus looked as lonely and miserable as she felt.

On the third day she offered him what she thought was an olive branch.

"We talked about going to the fair this week," she said. He looked at her in surprise. It was the first sentence she had spoken since their awful fight. "I wondered if you want to go with me today. Kitty and Dante are home for a long weekend, and they want me to go with them."

He wanted to go. The fair was a big deal in their community, and he had never missed going at least one day, but he had a lot of work to do.

"I don't think I can make it today," he said reluctantly.

Her anger at him was too fresh to register his reluctant tone. "Let me guess; you have work to do. I really hope by the time our children arrive you learn to delegate."

That stung. She should know better than to use their future children against him, he thought. "If you don't learn to control your paranoia over my mother we'll never get the chance to have any," he said.

"That's for certain," she agreed, and turned away before he could see her tears. The quick turn made her head spin and she stood still a moment to steady herself. "I'm going to the fair with my brother and best friend. Don't wait up," she said, storming from the house.

It was a hot day, which was to be expected in August, but for some reason the heat was bothering Cecily more than usual.

"Can we walk slower?" she asked Dante and Kitty. "You guys are sprinting today."

They looked at each other and smiled. "We may be a little bit excited this morning," Kitty said demurely.

Cecily stopped and grabbed her sleeve. "What? So help me spit it out and don't beat around the bush, either of you."

Kitty's face turned radiant. "Dante asked me to marry him last night." She linked her arm through Dante's and squeezed.

Cecily started to cry, great heaving sobs so that Dante was forced to lead her off the path and hug her tightly. "I thought you would be happy," he said.

"I am," she said between sobs. "That's why I'm crying, dummy."

Dante looked at Kitty over Cecily's head for some clue. Cecily was freer with her emotions than she was, but she didn't usually burst into hysterical weeping.

"Tell me all about it, every detail," Cecily said when she finally composed herself. "Let's sit down. It's too hot to keep walking." She sat and fanned herself for a minute before turning to her brother. "Will you get me a soda, please?" He ambled off and she turned back to Kitty. "Okay, I got rid of him so you can tell me all the good stuff."

Kitty grinned. Her best friend knew her well. She would have edited if Dante stayed. "He took me to the woods."

Cecily interrupted. "Don't tell me he took you to the shack where you guys were abducted."

"No," Kitty said. "Although I probably would have found that funny. This was much more romantic. He took me to this little shack that Maggie and Mathew built a long time ago." She paused, a pained expression flitting across her face. Maggie was still living in New York and trying to come to terms with Mathew's loss. "Anyway, it's sort of a special place. All of my sisters and our love interests have our names carved in the shack. We think of it like a wishing shack."

"I never figured you for a romantic," Cecily said. Kitty was as practical and down to earth as they came.

"You figured wrong," Kitty said. "So anyway, he gave me this big speech about how he had been in love with me for most of our lives, quoted Shakespeare, and then asked me. It was beautiful." She smiled dreamily.

Cecily smiled, too, thinking of the way Marcus had proposed to her. It hadn't been as eloquent or well thought out, but she wouldn't have it any other way. Suddenly she missed him like a fist to the gut.

"Did you by any chance bring your cell phone?" she asked Kitty.

"Yes," Kitty said. She had bought a cell phone for the first time when she left for college, and she still carried it out of habit. It didn't work on the ranch, but there was a cell tower in town. She handed it over with a knowing smile. "Missing your husband? It still feels weird to say that."

Cecily nodded and motioned to Kitty that she would be back in a moment. She walked some distance away so she could talk privately, but it went to voicemail.

"Marcus, I wanted to tell you I'm sorry for my whole part in our disagreement. I love you. I miss you, and I hope you're having a good day. Tonight I would love it if we can spend some time making up." She closed the phone and stared at it, disappointed she hadn't been able to talk to him in person.

The day felt more pleasant after that. She felt like she had done her part in putting things right between them, at least.

"You know what's odd?" she told Dante and Kitty.

"What?" they asked in unison, and then smiled at each other.

"No one has congratulated me on my marriage," she said. Theirs was a small, tight knit community. She knew almost everyone she encountered at the fair.

"That is weird," Kitty said. "Maybe no one knows about it."

"But how would that be possible? I mean, this is possibly the most gossipy place on earth, unless…" *Unless someone purposed to keep it hushed up*, she thought. Would her mother-in-law stoop to that level to hurt Cecily? Or was she being paranoid as Marcus accused her?

From then on everywhere they went she flashed her large diamond and platinum ring, and without fail she got the same response.

"Did you get engaged to that friend of Dante's?" people asked. "You know, the one with the weird name."

She didn't have the heart to spread her own gossip, so she simply shook her head and left them wondering.

"Someone call Guinness," Dante said. "This is one for the record books. The biggest event of the decade in our town and absolutely no one knows about it."

Cecily tried to laugh with Kitty, but inside she was deeply hurt. Come to think of it, she should have known. After all, they hadn't received any gifts and no one had mentioned holding a reception for them. That alone was unusual. She had been so blissfully happy that she hadn't noticed the lack of congratulations until now.

She could no longer hold in her hurt and her tears boiled over once more.

"Cecily, really, what is the matter with you?" Dante asked as he put his arm around her and gave her a one-armed hug.

She shook her head. Her pride wouldn't allow her to tell him. "I've been working hard at the ranch. This is the first day off I've had in a while. I guess I'm more tired than I thought." That was true. She did feel tired. Exhausted, even. She felt like she could curl up in the bed of their truck and take a long nap.

On top of that she felt badly that she was dragging Kitty and Dante down and raining on their parade.

"You are doing no such thing," Kitty scolded after Cecily apologized to her. "You're our family and we love you, even when you're exhausted and emotional and have to stop at the bathroom every twenty minutes." She froze.

Cecily froze, too. "I've been drinking like a fish," she said. "It's a million degrees out here. And I *have* been working hard, and it's made me exhausted." She glanced at Dante looking at a display. She lowered her voice. "And Marcus and I had a huge argument and haven't been speaking for a couple of days. I'm feeling emotional about that, I guess."

Kitty nodded sympathetically and looked relieved. If Cecily and Marcus were having problems, they certainly didn't need to add the complication of a child into the mix. "Do you want to talk about it?" she asked. "You know I won't tell anyone."

"I don't know," Cecily said. She was still feeling her way as a bride. She didn't want to share personal things that were between her and Marcus, but she had always confided her problems to Kitty. "Let me think about it awhile. I don't want to do anything to make things worse."

Kitty squeezed her arm. "That sounds wise."

Cecily grinned. "For a change, you mean. Go ahead and say it; I dare you."

"I wouldn't dream of saying that. To your face," Kitty added under her breath, and laughed hysterically when Cecily pinched her waist. Kitty was ticklish.

By the end of the day Cecily was hot, exhausted, and ready to go home to her husband, but there was a dance that night and she knew Kitty and Dante wanted to stay for it. She contented herself by standing on the sidelines and watching the happy couples dance by.

"Want to have a go at it?" a familiar voice asked.

"Oh, hello, Jessup," Cecily said. She smiled faintly. "I see they let you out of the barn today."

"Barely," he said dramatically. "You didn't answer my question. Want to dance?" He gave her what was probably his most practiced and endearing smile, but she was immune to his charms. She didn't care for a man who would hit on a married woman, if that was what was doing. It was difficult to tell because he was subtle.

"I don't think I have the energy for it," she said, which was true. But the main reason she refused him was because she wouldn't touch him with a ten foot pole. She was too well aware of Marcus's jealousy to so much as glance at him on most days.

"You do look a little worn out," Jessup said. He studied her with a worried frown that was far too possessive for Cecily's taste. "Let me buy you a soda."

She was parched and thought a soda seemed innocent enough. "That would be great, thanks. Something without caffeine, although as tired as I feel I doubt it will matter much tonight."

He smiled and ambled off to retrieve her drink.

He returned and she sipped at it gratefully. "Thanks," she said. She turned her attention back to the dancers and he did, too. She wanted to ask him why he wasn't here with someone, but she thought that might hint at too much interest on her part. She was curious about him, but in the way she was curious about everyone she met. She liked to know people's stories.

She took another sip of the soda. She had been too warm to eat much at supper, and now she was paying the piper. Her stomach was full of sugar and protesting.

"Excuse me," she said, turning to find a restroom. She turned too quickly and swayed on the spot. Jessup's arm's reflexively shot out to catch her. It was her bad luck Marcus chose that moment to find her.

"You're going to want to take your hands off my wife now," he said in a barely controlled manner Cecily had never heard him use.

Jessup, however, wasn't intimidated, even if the man speaking was his boss. "Then you'd better put yours on her because she's about to fall over."

Marcus's look changed from one of menace to alarm. "Lee?" he asked questioningly.

"I'm all right," she said shakily. "I had too much soda and not enough dinner, and the heat got to me." She lightly shook off Jessup's hands from her upper arms. "Thank you," she said, politely but stiffly.

"I think I should get you home," Marcus said, and his voice was once again cool.

She nodded. She really wasn't feeling well. "I need to find Kitty and Dante."

"I'll find them with you," he said. He put his arm around her and led her to where her brother and best friend were dancing.

"Hey, about time you showed up," Dante said cheerfully, oblivious to the tension between them. "Your wife has been a lonely, weepy mess without you."

That softened Marcus somewhat. "She was with you all day?" he couldn't help but ask.

Cecily blushed crimson at the assertion and jerked out of his grasp.

"Yes," Dante said warily. He had no idea what prompted the question or his sister's reaction to it.

Marcus nodded, feeling foolish now. "I think she's not feeling well. I'm going to take her home. I hope we'll see you again before you leave." He put his arm around Cecily and had to clamp it there when she tried to pull away from him again.

By the time they reached his truck she was struggling again, but this time with more urgency. He finally let her go and watched as she ran to a trash can and heaved into it. He came to stand beside her and held her hair away from her face.

"Come on, sweetheart, let's get you home." He bent and swept her into his arms before carrying her to the truck.

She was sick and miserable and tired and she started to cry. Loudly. "I wasn't with Jessup," she said brokenly. "I only saw him a second before you showed up. He bought me a soda because I was sick."

He deposited her in the truck and stood beside her, unable to move away even for the short time it would take to get to his side of the vehicle.

"I know that in my head, Lee, but when my heart thinks of you with another man, I go crazy. I'm sorry. For everything."

She pulled him close and wept against his neck. "I love you so much, and I missed you like crazy, and I'm going to throw up again." She moved away and held out her arms to him. He lifted her down and held her hair again while she threw up. She leaned against the truck and he pressed a worried hand to her forehead.

"I hope you didn't get dehydrated today," he said.

She shook her head. "I drank a lot. I had too much sugar on an empty stomach. It happens to me almost every time I go to the fair. I get sick if I don't eat properly." She grimaced. "It's embarrassing to have you see me like this."

He chuckled. "We're living up to our vows, baby girl. Do you think you can make it home now?"

She nodded, but she still felt uncertain. "At least I'll try to give you advanced warning before I get sick."

"That's all any man could hope for," he said, feeling somewhat reassured when she gave him a wan smile.

CHAPTER 23

Cecily woke feeling refreshed the next morning, and she was more relieved than she wanted to admit. For a moment she had feared she was pregnant. In the back of her mind she realized she hadn't started her period, but she had never been regular, so she shoved her worry away.

Marcus stayed nearby to make sure she was all right.

"I'm fine," she told him. She pressed her palm to his cheek. "Thanks for taking care of me." He leaned in to kiss her but she dodged him. "I need to go brush my teeth a few dozen times. Hold that thought." She grinned at him as she skittered away. When she returned he was lying in their bed fully dressed with his arm behind his head.

"Have I ever told you you're the handsomest man on the planet?" she asked. She crawled in beside him and pillowed her cheek on her hand.

He turned toward her and copied the pose. Her dark hair fell over her face like a curtain and he swept it aside. He loved her so much, this girl turned woman, stranger turned wife.

"What do you say we spend the day together?" he asked.

She sat up excitedly. "You mean it, Marcus?"

He nodded and smiled, glad that such a little thing could make her so happy.

Her smile dimmed and she froze. "I remembered my foreman is off today. I have to go to the ranch, at least for a little while."

He caught her hand and wound their fingers together. "I'll go with you. It's time I saw what you're up to over there. I'm ready whenever you are."

"Oh, I think we have a little time," she said. She leaned across him to turn on the radio, and then she kissed him.

Later he drove to her ranch in his truck. "I worry about you driving this route every day when winter hits, Lee," he said. "I didn't think you were going to have to go every day."

She didn't have to go every day; three times a week would suffice. But if she didn't go then she was stuck in the house with his mother, and risking an accident on the road seemed a much better solution, at least to her.

"I like to be busy," she told him, which was true. She had always been a high energy person.

He picked up her hand and kissed it. "Some day our kids will keep you busy."

Her stomach fluttered. It was still shocking to her that she would someday have Marcus Henshaw's baby. *The* Marcus Henshaw, she thought with a giggle.

He smiled, a knee-jerk reaction to her happiness. "What?"

She shook her head. "Nothing." It was too embarrassing to tell him her girlish delight at being married to practically the biggest catch in Montana. She squeezed his hand. "You could have had any girl you wanted, Marcus."

"I got the girl I wanted," he said. He winked at her and her heart melted. He was so…everything.

They arrived at her ranch but she made no move to exit the truck. Instead she slid over to him and wrapped her arms around his neck. "I love you," she said adoringly. At times she was so filled with love for him that she felt her heart might not be able to contain it.

He turned off the truck and took her in his arms. "What do you say you show me your old bedroom?" he said. "I don't think I've ever had the official tour."

She smiled and froze when the door to the house opened and Dante stepped out. "I forgot he's still here," she whispered. "Rain check."

"I'll expect interest on your payment," he whispered.

"You really are quite the businessman," she said.

He kissed her once more before helping her down out of the truck.

"This is a surprise," Dante said. "I expected to do all the work myself today since Ted's off." Ted was their foreman, an old cowboy who had been with them since before Cecily's birth. They counted him as family, especially since he had stood by Cecily when she could barely afford to pay him.

"Marcus is going to tag along today," Cecily said. "He's hoping to learn something about ranching." She grinned at him and hugged his waist. Along with many years of practical experience, he had a four year degree in agricultural business.

"Teach me your ways, oh wise one," he said lovingly, returning her hug.

"Don't be disappointed if you don't absorb it all today," she said, giving his stomach a patronizing pat. "These things take time. No one expects you to leave here an expert."

"You're a bad kid," he said. He squeezed her again.

Beside them Dante stood watching and smiling. The more time he spent with them, the better he felt about his sister's hasty marriage. To him Marcus Henshaw had always been the untouchable cool kid, one of the social elite who was above everyone else. He had worried that he would somehow feel superior to Cecily because she was poor as a church mouse compared to him, but what he saw made him happy. Cecily loved Marcus, and Marcus adored Cecily; Dante was sure of it. He never in a million years would have put them together, but now that he saw them work, he couldn't picture either of them with anyone else. And the more he thought about it, the more sense they made. They both loved the land and they were both hard workers. Marcus's even temperament balanced Cecily's flighty one.

"You look happy," Cecily commented to Dante.

He put his arm around her and squeezed. "I'm happy you're happy, little sister."

She hugged his waist. "I am. And I'm so excited for you and Kitty."

"Me too," he told her, and then let her go because he could tell Marcus was becoming jealous. *If you're jealous of me, wait until our dad gets out of jail,* he thought. Her father had always treated Cecily as his most prized possession. Dante was glad she and Marcus would be firmly established in their marriage before his release. That was one thing they didn't need to deal with right now.

Dante went about the normal duties he assumed whenever he was home. He wasn't adept at ranch life, but he had gotten better at it the past couple of years. Now he enjoyed the reprieve from his office job. *I'm probably the only actuary on the planet who's also a rancher,* he thought.

Cecily was in high spirits showing every facet of the operation to Marcus. Dante hoped his new brother-in-law was properly impressed. His little sister had reformed the ranch and made it profitable at a time when they were hemorrhaging money, and she had done it all on her own. He was certainly proud of her. He never knew she had it in her. If the ranch had fallen to him, he would have had it on the market and sold within the first month. The thought shamed him somehow and made him throw himself into his work with more gusto than usual.

For his part Marcus was impressed, both with his wife's innovation and her work ethic. "You have something good going here," he told her and smiled when she dimpled at him. "It was clever to think of raising horses. You're the only breeder for miles, and you're filling a need. Your business is going to boom once word gets out and your stock takes off."

"That's the plan," she said. "Although I can't say I thought that far ahead when I started. I was intent on survival, and I thought I had a better chance with something I knew. I tried to make a go of the cattle business." Her nose wrinkled. "It didn't suit."

She was a wonder, he thought. He had been born into wealth. He worked hard and he had made innovative improvements on the ranch that helped their business grow, but she had started with nothing. When she told him how close she came to losing everything, he was amazed at her grit.

"I think I must be a chauvinist because I constantly underestimate the female of our species," he said. "Women like you and Libby who make the most out of what life gives you." Libby had a keen sense for business, too. She sold jam in town and made a tidy profit from it. She also owned cashmere goats and sold their wool, along with sweaters she knit herself. Her business ventures had been a source of amusement to him during their relationship. He shook his head in wonder, not realizing that Cecily was now stiff and silent beside him.

At that moment Jessup emerged from the barn. He tipped his hat to Cecily and ignored Marcus. She hadn't known he was there; he came and went like a ghost most days.

"What was that about?" Marcus asked.

"What?" Cecily asked distractedly. Her mind was still on Libby, the wonder ex. How could she compete with a memory, and a perfect one at that?

"Jessup. Do you two spend all day together here?"

"What?" she asked again. She was taken aback by the frank accusation in his tone. "Marcus, are you crazy? I barely see him. I spend my days here alone. *Working.* Believe me when I tell you I am too busy and exhausted to do anything else." She crossed her arms over her chest. "You're certainly jealous and suspicious for someone who is carrying his own flame."

He scowled. "What are you talking about?"

"Please. I know you're not over Libby. You can stop pretending."

He put an arm out to stop her. "Lee, what are you talking about?"

Her eyes filled with tears and she dashed them away. "I know she was a paragon of perfection I could never hope to live up to. Your mother never wastes an opportunity to tell me."

His concern was overshadowed by his irritation. "Leave my mother out of this."

"Don't you think I wish I could?" she yelled, glad they were alone and too far from the barn to be overheard. "But I can't get away from her constant attempts to tear me apart, little by little. Every time I see her, I face an accusing scowl when all I'm guilty of is marrying you. I will never be good enough for you in her eyes because I will never be Libby. And the worst part is you agree with her."

"Lee, that's not even a little bit true," he said.

"Isn't it?" she asked. She dashed at her tears again, cursing her newly vulnerable emotions. "Libby would have been the perfect wife for you, or so I'm told. Repeatedly. She bakes, she cans, she knits, she always knows the proper thing to say and do. She doesn't cook paella with shellfish because she knows your mother's food preferences and allergies. She knows which pie is your favorite, and still bakes it for you, despite the fact that she's married to someone else. Everywhere I go, everything I do, I have the shadow of Libby hanging over me. And I see it on your face every time Libby is mentioned."

"You see what?" He was truly curious as to what she was talking about.

"That look. The 'why can't she be Libby look.' It's the same one your mother gives me, although she throws in a frown for good measure."

"That is unequivocally not true on both counts. Libby and I haven't dated in years. My mother knows she's married to Dobbie and having his baby."

"Much to her regret and yours," Cecily said. Her anger had fled and left her weak and broken. "Now everywhere you go you'll see a reminder of the baby that's not yours but should have been, isn't that right, Marcus?"

He stared at her in open-mouthed shock. How could she be so far off the mark? He couldn't believe her mind had conjured something so far from reality. Surely she was mistaken in her belief that his mother was encouraging these thoughts; no one was that cold-hearted.

"Lee," he tried. He reached for her but she wrenched out of his grasp.

"You can go," she said. "I have to take Dante to town today anyway so he can catch his flight tonight. Thank you for coming."

Her stiff, formal manner grated on his nerves. "Fine," he snapped. "Enjoy your day with Jessup." He tugged his Stetson further onto his head, slammed into his truck, and sped down the long driveway without a backward glance. If he had looked back, his heart would have softened at the sight of Cecily, weeping and alone with both hands pressed to her face.

CHAPTER 24

For the next couple of days the atmosphere between them was arctic. Cecily felt sick, body, mind, and soul. She hadn't meant to pour out her worries to Marcus or confess to him what his mother had been doing to her, but once she opened the bottle she couldn't contain what emptied out. Now he was angry at her, and hurt, and she didn't know how to fix it. On top of her original hurt Cecily now added the fact that he hadn't denied his adoration of Libby. And to make matters worse, he had defended his mother. In his eyes the woman could apparently do no wrong. As if to add insult to injury, Lydia was once again gleeful at the tension and distance between Cecily and Marcus. She also doted on Marcus by making all his favorite dishes and being more solicitous to him than usual.

Evan was her only ally, Cecily thought. He noted her wan complexion and lack of appetite with concern and remarked on it one night at supper.

"Cecily, are you feeling all right?' he asked. "You haven't been eating much, and you look tired."

"I'm fine, thank you," she lied. "How are the new bulls working out?" She didn't really care about the new bulls, but she didn't want to dwell on her own lackluster appearance.

He launched into a long discussion that lasted throughout dinner. Cecily was thankful for the opportunity to turn off her brain and listen to him for a while. Like usual, she offered to help Lydia with the cleanup, only this time she made sure to do it with Marcus in attendance.

"Why, yes, that would be nice," Lydia surprised her by saying.

Cecily was relieved to have something to do and had no energy to puzzle over the sudden turnabout until she was in the kitchen and overheard Lydia and Marcus in the dining room.

"That's a nice change," Lydia remarked.

"I'm sure she doesn't feel comfortable invading your territory, Mom. It is your house after all."

"She seems perfectly comfortable eating my food and relying on my hospitality," Lydia said. Her tone was injured.

"Hospitality?" Marcus echoed. "She's your daughter-in-law and you make her sound like a temporary houseguest."

Cecily knew she shouldn't eavesdrop, but she had nowhere else to go, and, try as she might, she couldn't tune them out. She was riveted.

"Isn't that what she is, Marcus? You have to admit you made a hasty decision that you are now regretting. Anyone with eyes can see that you two are unhappy."

"We're in the middle of a disagreement," Marcus said. "That doesn't equal unhappiness."

"You and Libby never argued like this," she said.

It sounded like Marcus slammed something on the table. "Mom, what are you talking about? Of course Libby and I never argued like this; we weren't married. Libby is married to Dobbie and growing larger with his child every day, in case you hadn't noticed."

"There's no need to be vulgar, Marcus."

"That is not vulgar, Mom, it's a fact of life. Libby is Dobbie's, not mine. Cecily is mine."

"Maggie is still available," Lydia said.

There was dead silence from the other room and Cecily held her breath.

"What are you saying?" Cecily was glad Marcus's tone conveyed all the shock she felt.

"I always knew one of you boys would end up with one of the Chapman girls. It's too late for Libby, but you can still marry Maggie. She could come home from New York. You can get your marriage annulled. You know Judge Roberts would do it if we asked him."

Cecily didn't wait to hear Marcus's reply. She couldn't. She set aside the dish she was scrubbing, dried her hands, and walked sedately to her horse. She couldn't care less that the sun was setting, and she ignored Jessup when he tried to talk to her. Instead she rode calmly to her house and let herself inside, not bothering to turn on any lights. She walked to her old room, curled up on her bed, and cried herself to sleep.

It was too bad she missed Marcus's reply to his mother because it would have gone a long way to heal the breach between them.

For a while he stared at her until she became uncomfortable and started to squirm. He realized, belatedly, that everything Cecily had told him was true. If his mother was saying these outrageous things to him, how much worse had she been to Cecily who was the object of her venom?

"Mom," he tried to keep his tone even and patient by remembering how deeply his brother's loss affected her. "Cecily and I could never be annulled, one of the main reasons being that our marriage has been consummated. Repeatedly."

She winced. He didn't mean to shock her, but maybe a shock was what she needed to see reason.

"Maggie was Mathew's. She wouldn't want me. Can't you see that would be painful for her? It's better for her if she finds someone else, someone not related to her dead fiancé. Besides that, she's a child. She's eighteen. That's eight years younger than me."

"That girl is six years younger than you," Lydia pointed out.

"By 'that girl' I'm assuming you mean my wife. She may be six years younger, but she's mature for her age. She's been standing on her own two feet and running her ranch for two years. Now listen to me, and listen to me good. I am in love with Cecily. I married her for that reason, and for that reason alone. I don't know why you refuse to see it, but Cecily and I are happy together. We suit each other. I know you're having a hard time adjusting to our marriage. I am sorry for the way it came about; it was never my intent to exclude you by going to Las Vegas. I was trying to protect you, and I wanted to be with her as soon as possible. But what's done is done. It's irreversible and the sooner you make peace with it, the better off we'll all be. If you can't learn to love Cecily, I expect you to at least be courteous to her." His hands were shaking by the time he finished speaking. His mother gave him a curt nod, which he returned, and then he exited the house and saddled his own horse.

He rode for hours until the edge of his anger and upset burned off, returning home exhausted. Cecily wasn't in the room, but sometimes she stayed up late talking to the horses. He showered and went to bed, falling into an exhausted, dreamless sleep.

It wasn't until the next morning that he realized Cecily hadn't slept beside him, and when he realized it, he jumped out of bed. His panic was immediate and intense, and when he guessed she went to her house, it turned to blazing anger.

If she thinks she can leave me barely three months into our marriage, she has another think coming, he thought as he angrily rammed his feet into his boots. He paused at the door to grab his Stetson and his keys, and then he was gone.

*C*ecily, on the other hand, woke up too sick to think anything at all. Her eyes popped open and she sprinted to the bathroom. She heaved into the toilet and sank to the ground beside it, shaking and weak. Her mouth felt like cotton so she opened the cupboard to search for mouthwash. She saw the pregnancy test she had purchased right after her honeymoon and froze. *Surely not,* she thought. She tried to count the days since her last cycle, but she couldn't remember. But they had been careful, she comforted herself, and then sat up in alarm. *Except that one time by the stream.* Now her heart, which had stopped briefly, was hammering double time.

She sank into a sitting position, pulled out the test, and read the directions. It said first thing in the morning was the best time, so she opened the test and took it. She washed her hands and made herself wait the requisite five minutes before looking. What she saw made her sprint to the toilet and throw up again. She was pregnant. She didn't need to open a second test to confirm what her heart and body were telling her. Somewhere in the back of her mind she realized she had known for a while now, but refused to allow herself to believe it.

Her hands shook as she threw the test away and tied it up in a bag so it wouldn't be discovered. That was all she needed, for Dante to see the box in the trash and learn her secret. She grabbed a washcloth, ran it under cool water, and pressed it to her forehead. Now no one would ever believe she hadn't gotten pregnant before her marriage. It was true that it hadn't happened until a month after her wedding, but most people wouldn't stop long enough to calculate the time difference. They would know a baby occurred less than a year after the wedding and assume the worst. Especially her mother-in-law. This would only add more fuel to the fire she had built against Cecily.

"So what?" Cecily said out loud. She threw down the cloth and banged the cupboard shut. So what if people talked about her? They were bound to gossip about her in some capacity anyway. Her only real worry was Marcus and his reaction to the news. As if thinking of him conjured him, she heard an insistent pounding on the door that could only be him.

"Oh drat it all," she yelled. In her haste to get away she hadn't told him she was leaving, and then she fell asleep before she could call. He was going to be livid, and rightly so.

When she opened the door, he stood on the other side looking thunderously angry for about thirty seconds, and then he threw aside his hat, picked her up, and kissed her breathless.

He had intended to yell at her, he really had. But when he caught sight of her standing in the doorway, fragile and sad and wearing her faded old nightgown with horses on it, and all he wanted was to hold her.

"You can't leave me, Lee," he said when the kiss was over. He gripped her shoulders tightly for emphasis.

"Marcus, I," she started, but he interrupted her.

"Let me speak. I'm sorry I didn't believe you about Mom. I had no idea she was as messed up as she is. In my defense that's not the same mother I've always known. I want you to forgive me, please, baby." He kissed her again and she clung to him tightly. The fact that she was carrying his child made her want to be closer to him, as close as she could get. That was why when he tried to let her go, she stood on her toes, kissing him again.

"I guess we're made up," he said lazily as they lay cuddled together that night.

She smiled against his shoulder.

"We need to talk about Libby," he said. She tensed, and he winced. He lightly traced his fingers down her arm until she relaxed. "I didn't believe you when you said my mother was holding Libby over your head. I knew she and Libby were close, but I thought she moved on when Libby and I did." He levered himself down so they were eye to eye. "Cecily, despite the fact that I proposed to her, Libby and I weren't that serious. She was what I thought I wanted, what I thought I needed to make the ranch a success, and so I pursued her. But I was in college and only saw her about one weekend a month. And, I'm ashamed to admit, I wasn't faithful to her. I was dating Lacey and a handful of other girls on the side. My mind wanted Libby, but my heart never did. I proposed to her because I was twenty two and grad-uating college. I panicked that I hadn't found 'the one.' Libby was sweet and pretty and already an excellent ranch wife. She's still all those things, but she's not mine, and she never has been. She never loved me, and I never loved her. I never loved anyone until you."

"You love me?" she asked, awed and overwhelmed.

"Of course I do. Why else would I have asked you to marry me?"

"But you never said," she told him. "I've been saying it every day and you never reciprocate."

"I do say it every day," he said sheepishly. "I wait until you're asleep."

She propped herself up on one elbow. "Why?"

"I may be twenty six, but that doesn't make me mature. I cheated on Libby. I cheated on Lacey. I thought for a while that was my nature. I didn't realize until I found you that it was because I was never in love with them and had no real desire to be with them." He took her hands and his tone became fervent. "Lee, do you have any idea how you've changed me? How you've altered my world? Two years ago I pulled you out of a bullpen, and you turned my life upside down. Suddenly all I could think of was you. I couldn't get enough of you. I still can't. I never will. I love you."

He pulled her into a crushing embrace, and she returned it, hugging him almost violently. She thought maybe she had never been happier. There were still things looming between them, though.

"Marcus," she began tentatively when the hug was over. "I don't think I can go back to that house with you knowing how unwelcome I am."

He expelled a long breath. "I know. I'm sorry I made you stay as long as I did. I really thought our presence there would help Mom heal. I'm afraid it only made things worse for everyone." As he talked he absently traced his hand over her, pausing at her stomach. He liked the feel of it, the way it was slightly and pleasantly rounded. All of her was soft, sweet, and pretty. Strange he had never dwelled on her stomach before. He leaned down to kiss it and she froze.

"How did you know?" she asked.

He pulled back to smile at her. "Know what?"

She blinked at him. He had to know. Why else would he be smoothing his hand over her stomach and kissing it? Was that why he was being so conciliatory? Was it all about the baby?

She wrenched out of his embrace and scooted away.

"Lee, what is wrong with you?"

"How did you find out about the baby?"

She knew by the way his face turned the color of rice paper that he didn't know.

"The baby?" he choked. His arm was still outstretched toward her.

She swallowed hard and moved under his hand again. She pressed it to her stomach. "The baby. Our baby. I'm pregnant. Surprise." She tried to sound cheerful, but she was uncertain. She had no idea how he would react to the news.

He stared at her, unblinking. "But you said we didn't get pregnant on our honeymoon."

"We didn't. Remember that day by the stream?" She tried to smile, but his lack of reaction was making her nervous.

She didn't have to wonder what he was thinking for long,

however. He tackled her and knocked her from the bed onto the soft carpet, using his arms as a shield to absorb the impact. "If it's a girl, can we name her River?" he asked, and then he kissed her, not waiting for an answer.

They slept fitfully that night, waking up off and on to cuddle and talk, mostly about the baby. They were staying in the guest room of her parents' house. Her parents' room had a king-sized bed and private bathroom, but she felt strange about sleeping in their bed.

"We'll get a new bed as soon as possible and then we can move in there," Marcus murmured drowsily as they were finally falling asleep.

"I like this one," she said.

"It's a double," he said.

"I like to be close to you," she told him.

He smiled. "Talk like that will get you pregnant."

"Too late," she said. She pressed her palm to his cheek. "How did it go when you went home to get your things this afternoon?"

"It was all right. Mom was subdued. Dad was the same, although when he helped me carry things to the truck he said he thought we were doing the right thing. And he said he's worried about Mom. He's never seen her act like this, either."

Cecily nodded. That was some small consolation she supposed. "You didn't tell them about the baby?"

He shook his head. "It's our secret for now."

"Our secret," she agreed. She bit her lip. "Marcus."

"Hmm." He was half asleep already.

"I wasn't leaving you. I came here to clear my head and I fell asleep. I would never leave you."

He smiled. When he spoke his voice was barely audible. "Doesn't matter. I would never let you go." He clasped her hand, and then he fell asleep.

CHAPTER 26

For the next month Marcus and Cecily lived at her ranch. For Cecily it was undoubtedly the happiest time of her life, despite her daily morning sickness. Life was the way she always dreamed it would be when she was a little girl and played house. Marcus left for work early in the morning and came home for supper while she puttered around the house and tended to her own duties. He had put his foot down about her level of work, but she didn't argue with him. She wanted the baby to be healthy, and she wasn't about to take the chance of injuring herself on the ranch.

Jessup started showing up more to help out, and between him and Tim, they were able to do the physical work while she took care of the business end of things. Marcus wasn't jealous of Jessup when he realized how little time he and Cecily actually spent together. It turned out that the other man had a serious girlfriend who lived in Billings. He and Marcus were now on their way to becoming good friends, and Marcus appreciated having him around to keep an eye on Cecily.

After keeping the news of her pregnancy a secret for an entire month, they finally told their families. Her mother was excited, more excited than Cecily would have guessed, and so was her father. She decided to use his excitement to tell him what she had been up to on the ranch in his absence.

"Guess what, Daddy?' she asked during his weekly call.

He caught the excitement in her voice and matched it. "What, little girl?"

"You're going to be a grandpa."

He paused in astonishment before whooping for joy. "All right! Looks like those Henshaws are really coming through." He laughed again and she tried to slip in her next information unnoticed.

"Also, I sold all your cows and bought horses."

Dead silence.

"You did what?" All traces of his earlier joy and excitement were gone.

"I tried to make it work with the cows, Dad, honestly I did, but I had no taste for it. I love horses, you know that, and the new business is going well. I'm actually starting to make a tidy profit."

"Define tidy," he said.

She told him what she made in the last few months.

He was silent again. "Was that your income for all of last year?"

"No. That was last quarter."

To her surprise he whistled appreciatively. "Let's tell people you got your business sense from me and call it even."

"Deal," she said. She would never in a million years tell him her biggest jump in earnings came after Marcus's dad gave her helpful advice.

"Speaking of which, did you know your mother has some fool notion that I'm going to Chicago with her after I get out?"

Cecily paused. Always before she had taken her father's side in any disagreement. It was time to change that. "Dad, Mom lived here on the ranch with you for a long, long time, and you know she hated it. A change of scenery might do you good, and I think you'll like Chicago. It has all the amenities of a city with a small town feel."

Her father took a long time in answering. She wondered if he was angry, but when he finally spoke he sounded thoughtful. "Maybe so," he said. "I guess I have a long time to decide either way."

They talked for a few more minutes before disconnecting. She called Dante and Kitty, sure they would be together. They were, and they were elated over her news.

After she hung up with them she sat nervously twiddling her thumbs until Marcus arrived home from telling his parents. She hadn't seen her mother-in-law since they moved out, partly because she was hurt and angry over the whole situation, but mostly because they thought it might help Lydia become more comfortable with the situation if the two women spent some time apart.

She heard his boot steps on the porch and knew by their heaviness that things hadn't gone well.

"That bad?" she asked when he stepped inside.

He held out his arms for her and she snuggled close to him. "Worse than I could have imagined."

"Tell me."

"At first she flew off the handle and started accusing us of jumping the gun again. I tried to reason with her and tell her you weren't far enough along for that, but she didn't believe me. Then it was like a switch was flipped and she blocked the whole thing out. She pretended I hadn't spoken. As far as she's concerned there is no baby."

Cecily smiled through her hurt. "Boy won't she be surprised in six months."

He gave a half-hearted smile and kissed her. "I'm worried about her. I tried to talk Dad into getting her professional help, but you know how it is. Henshaws don't get counseling." He shook his head. "I have a feeling something bad is coming."

She shivered. Marcus was usually level-headed and practical. To hear him talk of impending doom made her feel insecure at a time when she needed security most. "It's going to be all right," she said to reassure herself more than him. She hugged him close and pressed her face to his chest.

"*We'll* be all right, no matter what," he said. "Lee, I know I didn't do a good job of making this clear in the beginning, but if it comes down to a choice between you and my mother, I'll always choose you. You're my wife, and I love you."

She appreciated his words, but at the same time they made her sad. Since Mathew's death his parents were all the family he had. He shouldn't have to choose between her and them. She never wanted to put him in that situation. She wanted to fix things, but she had no idea how.

For the next two months they lived at her ranch and enjoyed newlywed bliss. After the first few tumultuous months living with Marcus's parents, Cecily found every day alone with him to be a luxury. She delighted in cooking supper, doing his laundry, and cleaning the house. He was always appreciative of her efforts in the kitchen, especially when she shyly presented him with a peach cobbler one night.

"Did I ever tell you I like cobbler better than pie?" he asked.

She thought maybe he was lying to make her feel good, but she didn't care. She pelted his face with kisses to show her appreciation.

Without the stress of his mother and her many hours of work, there was very little for them to argue about. Mostly they bickered about the things many newlyweds do, like where to keep the towels and how to fold them. Marcus was particular about his laundry, but after Cecily pointed out he could learn to like it her way or do it himself, he conceded the point.

Her stomach grew exponentially on an almost weekly basis. Their small town didn't have an obstetrician, so she had to drive two hours to reach one. Marcus didn't want her to drive that far by herself once a month, so he always took that day off to go with her. They usually made a day of it and spent time eating out, catching a movie, or shopping.

"I bet we're the only couple in history to start dating *after* we're married and pregnant," he said.

They were both nervous and excited as they went for their twenty week ultrasound.

"Today's the day we find out what's in there," Marcus reminded her, as if she could forget.

"What do you want?" she asked for the hundredth time.

"A baby." He always gave the same answer.

"That's wishy/washy," she said. "I want a boy, and then a girl. Every little girl needs a big brother."

"And then I want two more boys and another girl," he said. He pounded her lightly on the back when she choked on her orange juice. "Don't look at me like that. You knew when you married me I wanted five kids."

"I did not," she said when she could talk.

"That's really the sort of thing you should find out before you marry a man. I don't think I should be punished for your careless lapse." He gave her what she had come to call his bad-boy grin.

"You misunderstand me," she said sweetly. "I was upset because five is too few. I want at least eight."

Now it was his turn to choke. He sputtered until she winked at him to let him know she was teasing. He grinned at her again and took her hand. "How many do you really want?"

"Four," she said.

"Four is a nice round number," he said. "I can live with four. Why do people say marriage is hard? Apparently they don't know how to compromise."

She giggled. Something told her life wasn't always going to be this easy, so she decided to delight in it while it was.

To their disappointment the baby kept his or her legs crossed during the entire exam, so they weren't able to find out the sex. As a way to uplift their disappointment they decided to go shopping and buy a few baby things. Their local town had a baby store, despite the lack of a doctor who could deliver babies. They both liked to buy locally when they could, so they stopped there on the way back from the doctor.

As soon as Cecily stepped out of the car she felt like every eye was on her and Marcus.

"Why is everyone staring at us?" he asked.

"Oh. I forgot to tell you. No one knows we're married."

He smiled at her, sure she was teasing him. "Right. In this town? People knew I broke up with Libby before I did. There are no secrets here."

"I'm telling you, no one knows we're married." She didn't tell him what she suspected, that his mother had worked to keep things hushed up.

He smiled and shook his head at her. "Crazy girl."

"Fine, if you don't believe me, ask around."

"All right," he said. He took her hand and led her to the local diner.

"Hello, Marcus, Cecily." An older woman named Bee greeted them. Her eyes fell on Cecily's stomach and bulged.

"Bee, settle an argument between me and my wife," Marcus started, but Bee interrupted him.

"Your wife," she exclaimed. She pointed to Cecily. "Her?"

"You didn't know?" Marcus sounded truly incredulous. Cecily smiled smugly.

Bee shook her head. "How long, uh, have you been together?" She stared at Cecily's stomach. The implication was obvious.

"We've been married for seven months. Cecily's five months along," he stressed.

Bee nodded. "Congratulations," she said uncertainly. "Wow, I can't believe I haven't heard about this already. You'd think it would be big news." The excitement in her eyes told them it was about to be very big news, indeed. Bee was a legendary gossip.

Marcus didn't try to pretend she wasn't. "Make sure people understand we were married first," he said.

Bee nodded. She didn't try to pretend she wasn't going to spread the news as fast as chicken pox.

"Why don't you come to our table when you get a chance, and we'll tell you the whole story," Cecily offered.

Marcus was giving her a look, but she pinched his arm.

"Why are you going to tell her our business?" he whispered when they were alone at their table.

"Because if she doesn't know the story she's going to make something up. I'd rather her hear the truth from us. And if we give her an exclusive she'll go softer on us."

"You make her sound like a reporter for the *New York Times*."

"More like the *National Enquirer*."

"My wife is smart," he said. He leaned over the table to give her a sweet, affectionate kiss. More people than they realized were watching them at that moment. Until then people had been skeptical of the match, but Marcus's spontaneous kiss was an effective convincer. That combined with the sweet love story Bee spread soon had the town buzzing about the spectacular romance between *the* Marcus Henshaw and pretty little Cecily Blake.

CHAPTER 27

One month to the day after their ultrasound Marcus let himself in much earlier than usual.

Cecily knew by his footfalls that something was wrong. She hurried to the door as fast as her newly large size would allow.

"What's wrong?" she asked. She clutched her hand over her heart because his face was ashen.

"Maggie Chapman returned home yesterday. She's married."

"She…What?" Surely that couldn't be correct. Maggie and Mathew had been together for years and she adored him. How could she have married someone else so soon after his death?

Marcus nodded and ran a weary hand over his face. "It's a long story. Anyway, when Mom heard about it she flipped out. I wasn't there, but Dad sounded scared when he talked about it. I've never seen him scared of anything." He paused and swallowed down the deep emotion that choked his throat. "Somehow in the struggle of Dad trying to calm her she fell down a few stairs. She broke her ankle." He sat down heavily.

She sat next to him and put her arms around him. "I'm sorry, Marcus. I know it's hard to see her this way."

"I haven't told you the worst part. She asked for Libby to come and stay with her while she recuperates. I tried to explain to her that Libby's baby is due practically any minute, but she refused to accept the fact that Libby is even pregnant. It's like she can't see reality anymore at all."

Tears were her constant companion these days, and now was no exception. She hated to see him hurting, and hated even more that there was nothing she could do to fix it. She pulled him against her and cradled his head to her chest while she ran a soothing hand down his hair.

"We'll go," she said.

"What?" he asked. He didn't move away. She smiled because she knew he liked to be held and comforted this way, even though he would probably never admit it.

"Your mom is going to need someone to look after her and help around the house. I'm perfectly capable of housework. We'll move back in there and I'll help."

He did move away from her then. "Honey, the doctor said it was a bad break. It could take three months to heal. That would push you to your due date. I think we shouldn't put that kind of stress on you so close to the baby."

"How relaxed do you think I'll be knowing your mother needs help and we're not helping?" she asked. "She's our family and she's sick, in more ways than one. I'll be fine as long as you and I stick together."

Now he was the one to pull her close and cuddle her. "You're a treasure," he said lovingly. "I don't know what I did before you, and I certainly have no wish to find out what I would do without you."

She let him cradle her and think the best of her, but on the inside she knew the reality of what she was thinking. She would rather be horsewhipped than willingly place herself in her mother-in-law's reach again.

Nonetheless she put on a brave and happy face as they loaded up their things and moved back to the Henshaw's. They left the baby furniture, and when Marcus wasn't looking, she gave it a sad, wistful glance. She knew of course that she was still going to have the baby, and moving back in with her in-laws wouldn't change that, but things still felt like they were at an end, and that made her sad.

When they arrived at the Henshaw's ranch Lydia was sleeping. That was a relief to Cecily, but the house was still hushed the way it is when someone is seriously ill, or when there's been a tragedy. For lack of something better to do, she made decaffeinated coffee and set out a plate of cookies for Marcus and Evan.

They ate in silence and then Evan went to bed to check on Lydia.

"Come on, little wife," Marcus said after he helped her tidy up the kitchen. "Let's get you and the kid to bed."

She had to steel herself when they entered Marcus's old bedroom. Some bad times had taken place when they lived here, but some good times, too.

"The radio's still here," she remarked.

"Do you want me to turn it on?" He wagged his eyebrows at her.

She nodded.

He turned it on and she lay on her side facing him. She had always slept on her back and having to sleep on her side was uncomfortable. Marcus scooted down so his face was close to her stomach. An old country song played on the radio and he sang it softly to the baby.

Cecily smiled and pressed a hand to his head. Whatever happened the next few months she could face it, she thought. As long as she had him she could face anything.

She had no idea how quickly her thought was about to be tested.

The next morning a reluctant and worried Marcus finally left her to go to work.

"I'll be fine," she assured him. "She has a broken ankle. I can take her."

That made him laugh. "Like this?" He pointed to her protruding stomach.

"The baby will fight with me. He's very loyal."

He raised his eyebrows. "He?"

"Wishful thinking," she said.

"Then I hope it's a boy, because that's what you want, and I want you to be happy." He kissed her and left the house.

Cecily heaved herself up and exited the bedroom. She wasn't sure what to expect, but when she met up with Lydia in the kitchen she was her same, surly self. She was also standing at the counter pouring herself a cup of coffee.

"Lydia, please let me do that for you. I don't think you're supposed to be standing on your ankle."

Lydia stopped and turned to look at Cecily with a frown. "What are you doing here?"

"I'm here to help you," Cecily said hesitantly.

"I don't need your help," Lydia said.

"Evan and Marcus feel that you do. They're worried about you and want you to stay off your broken ankle until it mends."

"What about your precious ranch?"

"I can't exactly wrangle horses in this condition," Cecily said. "It's either housework or boredom, and I choose housework."

Lydia glanced at Cecily's protruding stomach and grimaced. "Fine, then. Whatever."

"Is there anything particular you would like me to do?" Cecily asked. She wasn't sure where to begin, and she didn't want to trespass.

"Don't you know how to clean?" Lydia asked.

Cecily tried to bite back a retort, but couldn't manage completely. "Fine, then, I'll start at the top as if nothing has been done so I'll know for sure I'm not missing anything. I'll also start on supper, so don't be surprised if you hear me rummaging through cupboards and the freezer while I make myself acquainted with your ingredients."

"We don't have any shellfish," Lydia said.

"I'll manage," Cecily said tightly. She used her mother's philosophy of cleaning, started at the top of the house, and worked her way down. She checked on Lydia frequently, but the older woman made no demands of her. Instead she watched television listlessly and without really seeing anything.

She took a break to make lunch, but Lydia barely picked at her food before returning to sit in front of the television. Cecily sighed as she cleared the table. She started on supper and decided to keep it simple. She made a casserole she knew Marcus liked, along with a salad and bread pudding for dessert.

The men ate heartily and complimented the food, but Lydia barely picked at it and didn't say a word. Cecily had expected to feel hostile resentment toward her, but she didn't. She felt sympathy. She was obviously sick and not because of her broken ankle. Her mind was sick as well. Cecily remembered how downtrodden she'd felt when her father was arrested and the ranch was in such trouble. She had thought she was facing the worst sort of misery then, but it was nothing compared to losing a child.

She would be patient with her mother-in-law, she determined. She needed love, care, and time. Eventually she hoped things would work out. Her hand went automatically to her stomach and she smiled faintly. Some people said babies were like magic. Maybe their baby would work a little miracle in this family.

CHAPTER 28

As the days wore on, Cecily's vow to remain patient, loving, and understanding became more difficult to keep. As Lydia adjusted to her presence she lost her listlessness and began to pick Cecily apart with a vengeance. Nothing she did was good enough for the older woman. Her cleaning wasn't sufficient, her meals weren't edible. The list went on and on.

At first Cecily tried to ignore her. When that became impossible, she tried using gentle rebuffs.

"If you don't like the way the roast tastes, what would you suggest to make it better?" she would ask. Or, "I don't see a ring around the toilet. When you're better and back on your feet, you can feel free to take care of anything I've missed."

Each night she fell into bed exhausted, both emotionally and physically. She was large and cumbersome. The baby pressed on her nerves, bladder, and lungs. Most days she felt nauseated and breathless. On her worst days, her sciatic nerve twinged painfully and she had to run to the restroom every twenty minutes. In addition to her physical misery, she was doing all the household chores for four adults. The laundry alone was staggering because ranch work was messy. Her back ached from carrying heavy laundry loads every day. On top of all that, Lydia insisted she give the house a thorough cleaning every day, including vacuuming. And their vacuum wasn't an upright; it was a heavy canister model that was awkward to use.

"Don't do it," Marcus chided. "Don't follow her every command like a whipped puppy. She has never cleaned every day; she cleans once a week. She's trying to break you."

"That's exactly why I won't quit," Cecily said.

"Honey, your pride is killing you," he told her as he rubbed her back.

"It's almost worth it to get you to do this," she said. He had taken pity on her discomfort and offered to give her a nightly massage.

"If you ever meet my fraternity brothers, I would appreciate it if you didn't mention this," he said.

She smiled. "I'll tell their wives. You'll be the envy of all of them. On second thought I won't. I don't need any more women to be envious of me."

"What other women? I don't see anyone but you," he said, and then he leaned down to kiss her.

The next day Cecily was bent over the bathtub, scrubbing, when her sciatic nerve sent a pain shooting down her leg.

"Oh," she exclaimed. She stood to rub it, but that didn't help. Sometimes walking did so she exited the bathroom to pace the living room.

"I never had as much trouble as that when I was carrying the boys," Lydia said.

Cecily's shock made her temporarily forget her pain. It was the first time Lydia had ever alluded to the baby in any way. "It must have been difficult for you having Marcus and being so far from your fami-ly." Lydia's family was from South Dakota, Marcus told Cecily. His father met her when he did business with Lydia's father.

"I had friends who helped me." Her eyes softened slightly and flashed hard again before she turned back to Cecily.

Cecily swallowed hard. "I'm glad we have family here. I want our baby to know his grandparents."

If possible, Lydia's eyes became even more malicious. "You're no family of ours. I hope your baby dies."

She couldn't have said what Cecily thought she heard, could she?

"Excuse me?" she asked. Her voice was barely a whisper.

"You heard me," Lydia said. "I hate you and that illegitimate spawn you're carrying. I wish you would both die."

There was no response to that, so Cecily didn't try. Instead she fled the house and went to the barn. She longed to jump on her horse and ride, but knew she couldn't. Instead she took one of the farm trucks and drove.

She had no conscious thought when she set out, but wasn't surprised when she pulled up in front of the Chapman's house.

Libby came out onto the porch to greet her, wiping her hands on a dishtowel.

"Hi, Cecily," she said cheerfully, despite the fact that she looked like she was about to pop any moment. "I heard you were expecting, too. I'm sorry I haven't had a chance to congratulate you in person. I'm almost two weeks overdue now, and Dobbie has a meltdown every time I try to set foot off the ranch." She smiled and rolled her eyes. "He's convinced he's going to have to deliver the baby, and the worst part is he thinks he can do it because he's delivered so many calves." She chuckled. "Men."

Cecily reached the porch and stood directly in front of Libby. And then she burst into tears. She had no idea what impulse brought her to the home of the woman Lydia had set up as her rival. Maybe it was because Libby was also pregnant and a sweet, loving person. Maybe it was sheer loneliness for the closest woman available. Or maybe she sensed that somehow Libby would understand.

Libby wrapped her arm around her and led her inside. They sat on the couch and Libby still didn't remove her arm. Cecily rested her head on Libby's shoulder and allowed herself to be comforted. Despite the fact that Libby was only two years older, it was Kitty who Cecily had been close to. Libby seemed much older than them because she had taken over the care of the house when her mother died. In some ways she felt like a surrogate mother to Cecily, or she had until she had been given reason to be jealous of her.

"Can you talk about it?" Libby asked gently.

"I don't know," Cecily said.

"Is it Lydia?" Libby guessed. She'd heard rumors, and she had her own suspicions from some of the strange comments Lydia had made to her.

Cecily's tears began anew and she nodded. "She h-h-hates me," she sobbed. After that the stopper was out of the bottle, and she poured out the entire story to Libby, including her unbidden part in it.

"Oh, Cecily, I'm so, so sorry. Lydia and I have always been close, but I had no idea she felt that strongly about things. And I never would have brought the pie if I'd known. I completely forgot it was Marcus's favorite. Dobbie's not a huge fan of peaches, so I find myself giving them away in any form I can."

"It's not your fault," Cecily said sincerely. She could absolve Libby of everything now that she was secure in the knowledge that Marcus didn't love her and never had. She sat up and wiped her face. "I don't know what to do, Libby. I've tried everything and then today," she had to stop and clear her throat. "Today she told me she wished my baby would die, and me along with it."

Libby gasped and covered her mouth with both hands. She shook her head. Her eyes were troubled. Cecily was glad her own horrified reaction hadn't been overblown. Maybe it was because they were both pregnant, but it was nice to have another woman understand how upsetting the comment was.

"You were only eight when my mother died," Libby said. "I know you wouldn't remember this, but she and Lydia were best friends. Lydia was lonely when she moved here from South Dakota, and my mom was also missing her family in Maryland. They struck up an instant bond and became as close as you and Kitty."

Cecily smiled faintly at the mention of her best friend.

"When we were really little, our families used to have play dates together, right up until the time my mom got too sick to do it. Lydia was a great friend to her then. She brought us meals and helped take care of us and the house. They used to joke that someday Marcus and Anne would get married, but of course Anne and Marcus butted heads all the time and she ended up dating Dobbie before Will came along. Anyway, Lydia was devastated when my mom died. I think she took it as hard as any of us. And I think a little part of her never lost the dream that in some way our families would unite. Anne was out of the running, but she had high hopes for me and Marcus, as you know. And she and I are a lot alike." Libby shook her head. "The Lydia you've described and the one I've seen since Mathew's death aren't the same lady I knew. Do you think it might help if I talk to her?"

"I don't know. I don't know what's going to help at this point, and a part of me thinks maybe it's me. Maybe she truly does hate me, regardless of her pain over Mathew's loss."

"I don't see how anyone could hate you, Cecily. We all love you, and so do Marcus and Evan. No, I'm convinced this has to do with Mathew. I think she's come unhinged in some way. I'm sorry. I wish I could do more, or offer you a solution."

"Maybe you could try talking to her," Cecily suggested. Libby had a soothing, gentle way about her. Maybe that alone would be enough to jolt Lydia out of whatever she was going through.

"I will," Libby said. "As soon as Dobbie removes the ankle bracelet and lets me out of the house." She spoke up and turned her head so the sound would carry.

Her husband, Dobbie, entered the living room and grinned at her. "You say the word, honey. I've got my calfjack ready. We can get that baby out in no time." He turned his eyes to Cecily. "Howdy, Mrs. Henshaw. Congratulations to you."

Cecily smiled at him. "Hi, Dobbie." He had a pleasant, easygoing nature and she had always liked him. Everyone had called him Dobbie for as long as she could remember. She wondered what his real name was and if Libby ever used it. He threw a hand over his shoulder in a wave and went back to the kitchen.

"He's all bluster," Libby said confidentially. "He puts up a brave front, but at the first contraction he's going to panic like a little girl.

I'm counting on Dad and Maggie's husband to get me to the hospital on time."

"What's the story with Maggie's husband?" Cecily asked, hoping she wasn't being too nosy.

"It's a long, crazy, story," Libby said. She sat back uncomfortably and told Cecily the entire story.

Cecily was enthralled and delighted to have something to concentrate on other than herself and her problems.

At the end of the visit the two women hugged and promised to stay in touch, and to set up a play date as soon as they and their children were ready.

When Cecily drove home she was smiling. Life was funny, she thought. For so many years Marcus had been right under her nose, and she had no idea she would eventually fall in love with him and have his baby. The same could be said for Libby. For so many years she had simply been her best friend's big sister, and now she was the closest thing Cecily had to a friend and confidant. She wondered what other surprises life had in store for her. Maybe it was selfish and immature, but she hoped they would all be good.

CHAPTER 29

Cecily didn't tell Marcus what Lydia said to her. It wouldn't change their situation, and it would only upset him and add stress to an already stressful situation. Instead she stifled her feelings, bit her tongue, and resumed working at whatever Lydia wanted.

She wondered if maybe it was working because Lydia was becoming more agitated. Cecily's theory was that she would eventually wear herself out when she realized her young daughter-in-law couldn't be defeated. While the theory worked well in her mind it was difficult in practice, more so because as the days progressed, Cecily became larger and more uncomfortable.

Lydia seemed to delight in her discomfort and never missed a chance to tell her how hard she had worked during her pregnancies, once even going so far as to say that she had helped Evan brand cattle in her ninth month with Mathew.

Cecily had been so disturbed and intrigued by the thought that she had asked Marcus about it. He laughed for a long time.

"That's what she told you? Honey, can you ever picture me allowing you to do that?"

"No," she said.

"And I'm liberated in my treatment of you, compared to my father.

He would never in a million years allow her to endanger herself in that way. In fact he hired a housekeeper with each pregnancy so Mom wouldn't work too hard."

"Really," Cecily said. She tapped her foot impatiently. "Interesting." She hadn't told Marcus any of the things his mother had been taunting her with lately. He was on her side, and she knew it. She had no need to make him more resentful of his mother, although he was becoming that way by watching his mother at supper.

"The meal is delicious, Mother," he snapped one night. "Cecily is a wonderful cook, and you know it. Stop complaining and eat your food."

"Don't talk to your mother that way," his father had said.

"Then tell her not to talk to my wife that way," Marcus said.

Evan kept silent. His son had a point.

The tension in the house was making Cecily crazy. She couldn't wait until it was over, and she was depressed that nothing was progressing in her relationship with Lydia, other than the other woman's hatred.

"The windows need cleaned today," Lydia said one morning.

Cecily sighed. The windows were the old fashioned kind that didn't tilt in for easy cleaning.

"I'll do what I can for the first floor, and I'll ask Marcus to clean the second floor," Cecily said.

"Never mind," Lydia said in the injured tone Cecily had come to dread. "I'll do it myself. I'm sure I can ascend the ladder with one good foot."

If Cecily thought she was bluffing she would have ignored her, but she knew her well enough to know by now that she actually would ascend the ladder with her broken ankle, if only to make Cecily feel guilty.

"Fine," Cecily said. She only hoped she could finish before Marcus arrived home because if he saw her on a ladder eight and a half months pregnant, he would most likely kill her.

She asked one of the stable hands to set up the ladder for her and then ignored his protests when she told him she intended to clean the windows.

"I'll do it for you, Ma'am," he offered pleadingly.

She wished she could take him up on the offer, she really did, but she knew how well that would go over with her mother-in-law; she had no desire to listen to a lecture on keeping the cowhands from their assigned duties by doing work that she, Cecily, was too lazy to do herself.

"I appreciate that, George, but I'll be fine, really. Thank you."

He stood back and studied her with troubled eyes, unsure of what to do. Everyone on the ranch knew of the terrible feud between the two women, and everyone knew of the outrageous tasks Miss Lydia was assigning to her daughter-in-law. Surely she wouldn't make a pregnant woman clean windows on the second floor, would she?

He debated with himself for another minute, and then he left to call Marcus.

Cecily cleaned all the windows on the main level first. They were her height, not very dirty, and easy to clean.

"Let's hope the second floor goes this well," she muttered. She took a deep breath and started to climb.

Marcus was in the far pasture when George called him. At first he laughed.

"There is no way my wife would be that stupid," he said. "She's very protective of our baby."

George paused, clearly uncomfortable in what he was about to say. "With all due respect, sir, your mother has been riding her pretty hard here lately, and it seems to be getting worse. She's said some not nice things that have carried into the barn and yesterday I saw your wife standing on a chair. It looked like she was dusting ceiling fans."

Cecily had been tight-lipped about what went on during the daytime. He hoped it was because she and his mother avoided each other. Now he wasn't so sure. "Is she on the ladder now?"

"No, sir. She's cleaning the windows on the first floor."

He let out a relieved breath. "I don't think she'll get on the ladder,

George, but thank you for calling all the same. Most likely she got it out for me and I'll clean the second floor windows when I get home."

"If you say so, sir," George said, clearly not convinced.

Marcus hung up, still feeling uneasy. As far as he was concerned he didn't even want Cecily to be cleaning the main level windows. If his mother had truly put her up to it, what had she been thinking?

He picked up his cell phone again and called his father. "Dad, I'm going back to the house to check on Cecily."

"I'll come with you," his father said. "I have a bad feeling about things."

Now Marcus's unease accelerated into panic. His father was even more level-headed than he was. For him to rely on a gut instinct spelled disaster in the making.

Sure enough as they pulled up to the house there was Cecily balancing her bulk on the top of a ladder.

"Glory be!" his father exclaimed.

"I'm going to kill her," Marcus ground out.

Cecily heard their truck. She turned to look at Marcus with a sheepish expression, but she didn't take into account her new center of gravity. She scrambled to hold on, and then she pitched backwards. She felt the unbearable weightlessness of dropping and then hit the ground with a terrible thud. After that everything went black.

CHAPTER 30

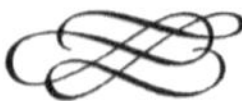

It's possible that Marcus cursed in that horrible moment when he saw his wife pitch off the ladder. He couldn't be sure because for a moment he went out of his head. All he knew was that when he reached her she wasn't moving, and there was a puddle of blood all around her.

His mother must have been alerted by the commotion because she came out to the porch, a frown on her face.

"What now?" she asked irritably.

"She's dead," Marcus yelled. "You killed her."

Her mouth fell open. She looked at the ground where Cecily lay and fell back against the doorframe.

"No, no, no, I didn't mean it. I swear I didn't. Oh, please, no."

Marcus would have raged at her again, but his father interrupted. He had always maintained a cool head in emergencies. So had Marcus, usually, but the sight of his wife unhinged him.

"Both of you calm down and be quiet," Evan snapped. They complied immediately with the authoritative tone in his voice. "She's not dead, but her pulse is weak and she will be if we don't get her some help. George," he called.

George came running. His face went white when he saw Cecily on the ground. "I'm sorry," he started. "I'm sorry. A calf got its head stuck in the feeder and I got distracted."

"Pull yourself together, man," Evan commanded. "I'm going to need the helicopter. I'm going to go start it. You and Marcus carry her behind me."

Marcus was thankful not only for his family's helicopter, but also that his father was giving him directions. He couldn't seem to think on his own. If he lost her…He and George carried her to the chopper in silence. There was so much blood. How would she ever survive? How would the baby? If she lived and lost the baby, a part of her would die with it anyway.

Tears ran unchecked down his cheeks. He only wished they would help ease some of the nightmarish fear and pain inside him.

"I'm sorry, I'm sorry, I'm sorry," his mother repeated over and over as she hobbled behind them.

"You should be," Marcus yelled as he laid Cecily inside the machine. "If something happens to her or our baby, I swear I'll never forgive you or speak to you again."

His mother put her hands over her face and wept.

"Come on," his father said impatiently. Marcus hopped inside the helicopter. His father kept him from looking at Cecily by instructing him to radio the hospital and tell them what they were coming in with. It was a good thing because if he glanced at Cecily and saw the life slowly draining from her face, he might jump from the helicopter to save himself the misery of losing her.

When they arrived at the hospital and she was put on life support he had to be sedated. He came to in a panic but tried to calm himself in case they threatened to sedate him again. He was in a bed and hooked to an IV, but he ripped it out and looked around for his clothes. He was beyond angry that his wife was critically injured and he was lying in a hospital bed because he had tried to take a swing at a few people when they took her away from him.

His legs were unsteady as he walked to the nurses' station. He wasn't sure what they gave him, but it had been potent.

"Where's my wife?" he asked.

A young-looking nurse looked at him in alarm. "Uh," she said.

"My wife," he practically yelled. His fist clenched and he banged it on the counter.

"Is your wife the pregnant one that came in on a helicopter?" A man Marcus assumed to be a doctor asked the question.

"Yes." He was relieved someone knew something, at least.

"Come with me," the man said. He turned his back and Marcus followed.

"What can you tell me?" Marcus asked desperately as they entered the elevator.

"Nothing." He held up his hands in supplication when Marcus advanced on him. "Because I don't know. She's not my patient. I only know of her because you caused such a stir by your arrival. I know it's hard, but you might try to calm down. You don't want to get in the way of your wife's care."

"She's still alive?" Marcus asked hopefully.

"I truly have no idea. I'm sorry. I'll try to get some answers for you."

The elevator door opened and Marcus followed the man to what was obviously a maternity ward. The doctor walked authoritatively to the nurses' station.

"This young man is the husband of the trauma victim. What can you tell him of his wife's condition?"

The head nurse was, thankfully, in attendance and piped up. "Right this way, sir. We'll let you see her. Your father hasn't left her side since the surgery."

He swallowed hard. He couldn't ask about a surgery or the baby right now. He simply needed to see Cecily and make sure she was all right.

When he entered and saw her hooked to every imaginable tube and machine he almost panicked and bolted again; Then he saw his father sitting sedately by the bed, looking tired, but calm and determined.

"She's alive," Evan said in his steady way.

Marcus began to weep with relief. She was alive. That was enough for now. They would deal with everything else as it arose. He walked to the bed and pressed a kiss to the only part of her he could safely touch, which happened to be her forehead.

"Lee, it's me, honey. Sorry I left you for a little while. I'm here now. I love you." He took a deep breath and turned to the nurse.

"I'll page her doctor for you," she said, and then left.

"They've been like that since I got here. You would think they're keeping state secrets," his father said irritably.

Marcus barely had time to become antsy and impatient before the doctor returned.

"We got lucky," were the doctor's first words. "When a woman is pregnant her body releases a hormone called relaxin. It makes her muscles, joints, and tendons looser, so no bones were broken. With a fall like that, there's often a fracture of the neck or back. The relaxin may have saved your wife, as well as your baby."

Marcus straightened. "The baby's alive?"

"Alive and well," the doctor said. "The fall sent her into labor and ruptured a few membranes. That was what all the blood was from. It was touch and go for a little while to see if she would hemorrhage after we took the baby, but we were able to get the bleeding stopped. He's only thirty five weeks, which isn't considered full term, but he's five pounds and so far very healthy. The main concern now is your wife's head. As you can imagine it took a pretty good jolt when she fell off the ladder. There's significant swelling, but the brain has an amazing capacity to heal itself. Her vitals are good and strong. For now it's going to be a waiting game as we watch the swelling go down. We put her in a coma so we can control her level of stimulation. In a few days we'll take out the breathing tube and slowly bring her out of the coma. At that time we'll know if there's any brain damage or not. We're going to keep her in the maternity ward overnight because the staff is more trained in dealing with a woman post c-section. Would you like to see your son?"

Marcus looked at Cecily. He wasn't sure he could leave her right now.

"I'll stay with her," his father reassured him. "Go see your boy."

That caught Marcus's attention. "Boy? It's a boy?"

The doctor nodded.

Marcus grinned. "Did you hear that, Lee? You got your boy, honey. Come back so we can get you your girl." He lightly squeezed her hand and followed the doctor to the nursery.

Holding his son was magical. He had never seen anything so tiny, pink, and beautiful. He had Cecily's dark hair and dark complexion. *And her temper,* he thought, as the baby opened its mouth to scream bloody murder. *And yours, too,* he could hear Cecily's voice chiding him. He smiled and dashed at his tears again.

"You can take the baby to see your wife," the nurse said. She looked around furtively. "It's not popular opinion, but I think people can understand some things when they're in a coma. Knowing the baby is so close might help her, or at least provide her some comfort."

"Thank you," Marcus said. He smiled at the woman and then carried his baby to Cecily's room.

His father sat up interestedly.

"Want to hold him, Dad?"

"Sure," his father said. "Don't look so surprised. I held you and your brother, didn't I?" He took the baby in his arms and smiled at him. "He looks exactly like her."

"She'll be disappointed," Marcus said. "She wanted him to look like me."

"She won't be disappointed at all," his father assured him. "I called your mother. She wants to come."

"I don't want her here."

Evan blew out a breath. "I can understand you feeling that way, but we both know your mother hasn't been herself. Seeing what she's done might cause her a world of good."

"Let me get through today, Dad, all right? I can't think about anything else right now."

"All right, son."

His father stayed a little while longer holding his new grandson, and then he flew home.

$\mathcal{M}$arcus didn't leave the hospital. His father brought him clothes and toiletries when he visited daily. And every day he implored Marcus to let his mother visit.

"She won't eat, she can't sleep. It's killing her to know what she did. I'm telling you, if you let her visit I think it might help. Please," he added.

It was the please that did it. His father was a proud man who usually didn't ask for anything.

"All right," Marcus agreed. "But if she says one negative word about Cecily or the baby I can't promise I'll be able to control myself."

His father nodded. *He looks old*, Marcus thought. Mathew's death, his mother's decline, and then Cecily's fall had taken their toll on him. That thought alone was enough to extend grace to his mother. He didn't want his father to suffer any more than he already had.

When she arrived he hardly recognized her. Gone was the hard, angry look she'd had lately, only to be replaced by confusion and fear. At first she had no idea who he was, but when she saw Cecily lying in the bed she came to and started to weep.

"Oh," she said, over and over again. "Oh, what have I done? What have I done?"

He swallowed down a lump. His mother had harmed his wife, but the woman before him wasn't really his mother. His mother was a gentle creature who would never hurt anyone. Mental illness wasn't her fault. He touched her shoulder and she jumped. "Do you want to see your grandson?"

She blinked at him in confusion. "I don't know," she said uncertainly.

"I think you'll like him," he said. He left to retrieve his baby, and couldn't help but smile as he presented him to his mother. Her face lit up and she actually smiled.

"Mom, meet Mathew Joaquin Diaz Blake Henshaw." He chuckled as she puzzled over all the names. He never would have given in to Cecily's bizarre name requests if she had been conscious—a fact which she would no doubt lord over him for all their lives.

"Mathew," his mother murmured, and then it was as if something within her snapped and she burst into violent tears. Marcus wondered if he should take the baby from her, but before he could his father cradled both her and the baby to him and held them securely in his grasp. In the end he was forced to turn away from the tender scene because it was too emotional, and because it made him desperate for Cecily.

His parents wept and rocked baby Mathew for a long time, but when it was over his mother had a new light in her eyes. There was clarity and some of her old familiar softness.

After that she was there as much as he was. She cuddled Mathew and insisted on feeding him whenever Marcus declined. Briefly he worried that she might lose her grip on reality again and think Mathew was hers, but his fears were dispelled when he saw her point to Cecily and tell Mathew it was his mommy.

Slowly Cecily was weaned off the drugs keeping her in a coma. The breathing tube came out and she seemed much more comfortable. When she finally opened her eyes, Marcus had just stepped out of the room to take Mathew back to the nursery. But Lydia was there.

Cecily winced, and the action brought tears to Lydia's eyes.

"It's all right," she said gently. "I won't hurt you. Do you know who you are?"

"Cecily Henshaw."

Lydia smiled because she had used her married name, despite the fact she was a newlywed. "Do you know who I am?"

"You're Marcus's mother," she said warily. There was something different about Lydia, but Cecily was too dazed to puzzle it together.

"Do you know what happened to you?"

Cecily tried to nod and then winced. She touched her hand to her throat. It hurt to talk, too. "I fell off a ladder." She closed her eyes.

"Yes," Lydia said. "You fell off a ladder and almost died because of me. Because I made you." Her voice broke on a sob. "Oh, Cecily, I'm so sorry. Can you ever forgive me? I behaved abominably."

"Why?" Cecily croaked. She opened her eyes.

"I was mad because my baby was taken away, and you came into the picture at the right time for me to be angry. I know it's not rational. I knew it at the time, but I couldn't control myself. I didn't want to say or do all those horrible things to you, but it was like I couldn't stop and in some weird way it made the pain a little bit better."

"Do you hate me?" Cecily asked. "Do you really disapprove of me for Marcus?"

"Oh, no," Lydia said. Her tone was so sincere that Cecily felt hope for the first time in her marriage. "I always thought you were a pretty girl, and I always admired your spirit. I'll admit your marriage took me by surprise and maybe in the beginning I did disapprove because of the age difference and because I thought you were flighty and immature."

"I was," Cecily said.

Lydia smiled. "Maybe when you were a little girl, but you've grown into a delightful woman. I couldn't think of a better partner for Marcus. And you're a good cook, too. When you get better I hope you'll make some more of those tapas. I almost ordered some off the internet because I've been craving them since I had them at your house."

Cecily laughed and it hurt.

"I'm sorry," Lydia said again. "I won't ever get over what I've done to you, what I almost did to you."

"I will," Cecily said. "You were ill. I forgive you."

Lydia started to cry, and so did Cecily, but at that moment Marcus entered and her face became radiant.

"Marcus," she breathed. He was next to her and kissing her before she could finish saying his name.

"I'll make myself scarce," Lydia said. She paused in the doorway to smile at the picture they made, and then she went to the nursery to see Mathew.

"Don't ever, ever, ever scare me like that again. I'm burning all ladders on the property and you're grounded until you're thirty."

"Where's Mathew? You don't know what sort of torture it was to hear him cry and not be able to hold him."

"You could hear him?" Marcus asked, a bit of awe in his voice.

"I could hear everything when I was awake, I couldn't communicate. Now go, go get our son, please, and hurry."

He went to do her bidding, thinking he had never enjoyed being ordered around more than he did at this moment.

The next day when Cecily was sitting up feeding Mathew, a light knock sounded on the door.

"Come in," Cecily called.

Libby and Dobbie entered, holding their new baby daughter. They named her Celia after Libby's mother.

"Is it all right if we have that play date now?" Libby asked.

"Perfect timing," Cecily declared.

"We had to bring Celia for her checkup, so we thought we would say hello. Meet your neighbor, Celia." Libby held up her little daughter next to Mathew.

"She's bigger than him," Dobbie commented.

"He was early," Libby said. "Give him time. He'll overtake her soon." She smiled mischievously at Cecily. "Wouldn't it be great if they got married someday?"

"Oh, no you don't," Marcus said as he entered the room. "Don't start that, Libby Dobbins."

"Amen," Dobbie said. "Let them make their own choices, especially about who they want to marry."

"Of course we will," Cecily said. "But we'll arrange it so they *want* to marry each other."

Libby gave her an approving smile while the two husbands groaned. Despite their joking, none of them could have predicted that almost twenty years to the day later Mathew Henshaw would in fact marry Celia Dobbins. But that's exactly what happened.

Thank you for reading *The Cowgirl Who Loved Horses,* the 5th and final book in the Queens of Montana series. For more books, please check out my website at www.vanessagraybartal.com